Hungarian Roulette

STEPHEN LISTER

Hungarian Roulette

PETER DAVIES : LONDON

Peter Davies Ltd
15 Queen St, Mayfair, London WIX 8BE
LONDON   MELBURG   TORONTO
JOHANNESBURG   AUCKLAND

Printed in Great Britain by
Willmer Brothers Limited, Birkenhead

I

Between the two world wars, after their country had been dismembered and virtually destroyed under the terms of the Trianon Treaty, young Hungarians with a spark of brains and initiative were not slow to realize that their native land had little to offer them. Hungary, there can be no doubt, was treated very harshly for the crime of guilt by association with the German arch-criminals.

The immediate consequence was that from the plains of Hungary, heading westwards, there began a mass exodus of the cream of Hungarian youth. Thanks to the excellent educational system, as well as to their own difficult language which nobody else could be bothered to speak, most of them were linguists, speaking German, Italian, French and English with great fluency if with an atrocious accent.

Streaming across Western Europe, the majority penniless or nearly so, they took with them a bewildering variety of skills and professional qualifications, a willingness to work hard, an almost miraculous adaptability and a determination that was frightening in its intensity. Architects, engineers, teachers, inventors, writers, musicians, journalists, cartoonists, spurred by necessity, they quickly found their niches in France, Germany, England, the United States, Canada and Australia, merging in an incredibly short time into the pattern of their adopted countries. Many of them prospered mightily, creating prosperity for others as they did so, exercising a profound influence on their times. It is not too much to say, before this turns into a politico-economic-ethnic hodge-podge, that seldom in history has such a numerically small group of talented men and women left such clear and lasting footprints as they went.

The first of these hungry Hungarians to cross my path was

1

a man named Josef Hegedus, who came to me seeking a job. I could not give him one, but I introduced him in turn to a friend named McIntyre, who imported alabaster lampshades and ornaments from Italy, expensive cigarettes from the Balkans. McIntyre soon afterwards sent me five hundred of these last as a token of appreciation. But on the last occasion we met, which was at the house of a mutual friend, he was barely polite to me. On receiving shortly after a circular from the firm of Hegedus & McIntyre I understood why.

During the years I remained active in the business world Hegedus sent several job-hunting compatriots to me with varying success.

Soon after the second world war I ran into Hegedus in Paris. He took me to dine at a Hungarian restaurant where the food was so incredibly horrible that it still crops up in nightmares. That, however, is incidental. The place itself and the atmosphere were delightful, and although all I could eat was bread and cheese with a heavy Hungarian wine, I thoroughly enjoyed the evening.

The restaurant was full of nostalgic Hungarians weeping as the orchestra played the haunting music of their homeland which, already, they were fairly sure they would never see again.

During the meal a young man crossed the room to speak to my host. His name—but I learned this later—was János Tisza. 'János,' said Hegedus when the former had returned to his own table, 'is a nice chap but a bloody fool. He is by way of being a mathematical genius. A dozen well-paid jobs could be his any time he cares to apply for them. He wants me to help finance him in a mad scheme. He has invented a roulette system which, he claims, will bankrupt the casinos.'

'Then I hope he fails,' I said, 'because I enjoy an occasional evening at roulette.'

Tisza seemed a pleasant chap and I found myself hoping that he would not be hurt too much by his inevitable failure, but I was appalled to realize that such an apparently intelligent man could be so crassly stupid as to suppose that

2

any mathematical system ever devised could constitute a serious threat to the well-entrenched casino interests.

It is well known that several 'systems' enable those with the patience to make a pitifully small steady income out of roulette. I believe they are nearly all dead now, but there were until a few years ago a handful of elderly Englishwomen —possibly other nationalities as well—scattered the length of the French Riviera, whose only source of income was roulette. The casinos, of course, were fully aware of this, just as they knew quite well that the minimum and maximum stake limits ensured that these poor souls could never be a danger. One of these old ladies whom I knew quite well before the war made an average annual income of about £180 from her system. In her best year she had once made just over £300, while in one year only she had made a small loss which had necessitated an appeal for funds from a wealthy relative. She and others like her were regarded by the casinos as good publicity, being the living proof that they were run honestly and that anyone with the patience to suffer the tedium of eight hours play seven days a week, to say nothing of the discipline required to adhere strictly to the system, could win consistently.

János Tisza managed to persuade a small syndicate to put up the equivalent of about £2,000 to finance his assault upon the casinos. I do not even know what his system was, being so out of patience with the whole thing that I did not listen when it was explained to me. Needless to say, it failed, and so far as his friends and acquaintances were concerned. János Tisza sank out of sight. This was, I judge from memory, in 1947 or 1948.

Some three or four years later I went to lunch in Grasse with a friend who had, not long previously, inherited a small but prosperous perfumery in the town. Arriving a little ahead of time, I joined a group of tourists being shown round the establishment. While passing a kind of laboratory filled with complicated apparatus quite unfamiliar to me, I caught a glimpse of a young man closely resembling János Tisza. Deciding not to make myself known to him, I completed the tour of the perfumery and joined my host, who was waiting for me in the entrance hall.

My perfumer friend, Pierre Morel, apologized for the fact that although Grasse was almost certainly the richest town of its size in France, it possessed no eating place of any distinction.

Pierre Morel was always interesting, which made the indifferent food unimportant. 'When I inherited this business,' he told me, 'I was out of patience with the old-fashioned methods employed, some of which have not changed for centuries. But when I attempted to modernize the plant and our methods, I was forced to admit that, clumsy as some of the processes undoubtedly are, I could not improve on them. So at length I sat back, as each generation of my family has done in the past, and carried on in the old ways. But recent developments suggest to me that big changes are on the way. . . .'

I waited.

'Last year,' he went on, 'I employed a remarkable young man, a Hungarian. I say remarkable because, if he continues as he has begun, he will end by being the oustanding *nez* in the entire industry. . . .'

'Outstanding what?' I exclaimed.

'*Nez*, what you call nose in English. I will explain,' he added, seeing that I did not know what he was talking about. 'The key personality in any perfumery is what we call the *nez*, someone whose sense of smell is as accurate as a piece of precision machinery. We rely on him for the proper blending of essential oils and other ingredients. Errors on the part of the *nez* are very costly and can be disastrous. This young Hungarian has learned in six months what some men learn in half a lifetime. I will say no more now, but when you see him in action you will be able to judge for yourself.'

After lunch, when we returned to the perfumery and I met the prodigy in Pierre Morel's office, I was not quite sure whether or not this was the János Tisza I had met in

4

Paris. He set my doubts at rest by recalling the occasion as soon as we were introduced.

'What does your nose tell you about this gentleman?' asked Morel.

'Oh, many things. For example, recently . . . not today or even yesterday, he has washed with a soap containing sandalwood oil. . . .'

Two or three days previously I had done so at a friend's house.

'His usual soap, I rather think shaving soap, is scented with rose geranium,' he continued. 'While I can see from the state of his clothes that he does not take snuff, he has today, or at earliest yesterday, been in contact with a snufftaker. He eats highly spiced foods . . . so much so that I am about to sneeze.'

Thereupon Tisza sneezed violently. 'There must be spilled pepper on your clothes,' he added apologetically. 'Now we come to something a little more difficult. Tell me, do you care for Chinese food?'

'No, I abominate it.'

'Then how, I wonder, to account for the odour of soy?'

'Soy is one of the ingredients of Worcester sauce, which French hôteliers call *Sauce Anglaise*,' I told him. 'I used a little at lunch with my lamb cutlets.'

'Ah!'

'A wonderful performance!' I felt compelled to say. 'I give you full marks. Go to the top of the class.'

I was glad to note that Tisza had evidently got the roulette system out of his own system, marvelling at the sheer versatility of this young Hungarian who in a few short months seemed well on the way to becoming indispensable in this ancient perfume industry.

'That young man,' said Morel when we were alone in his private office, 'has shown me how to use one-eighth the quantity of an essential oil costing more than three million francs [old francs, *bien entendu*] the litre, replacing it by an ingredient costing less than a twentieth part of the price, without debasing the finished product. If it turns out as I

5

believe it will, he has already saved me the cost of ten years' salary. These Hungarians! They have something. Added to everything else, he is by way of being a self-taught chemist.'

I thought it kinder not to mention that Tisza was also a roulette system hound.

Loudly as Morel sang Tisza's praises, I had a feeling that he was not entirely easy in his mind about the young man. It rankled with him that the other had apparently acquired in six months knowledge which many men needed a lifetime to acquire and even then some of them failed. 'We who have borne the heat and burden of the day.' Was it something like that?

What pleased me most about the encounter was to learn that I had misjudged János Tisza, who may have been foolish enough—surely the privilege of youth—to have believed that he had evolved an infallible roulette system, but had been spared the agonies which pursued a gambler to his grave.

2

In the little world which radiated from Grasse, the perfumery capital, as it has been called, János Tisza soon achieved fame. He had his detractors, too, which in a curious way added to his fame. The perfume industry, it seemed, operated in much the same way as the ancient English guilds, tight-sealed against intrusion by outsiders. Inevitably, his quick success caused bitter jealousies in this close-knit industry whose skills as well as ownership were largely hereditary.

I saw János Tisza several times in the months following my luncheon with Pierre Morel and found myself liking him more than ordinarily. The first meeting was in Ste Monique, the village which I have called home for more years than I care to remember. He was staying with some people, Belgian newcomers, whom I had not met. Then, to my horror, I met him one evening at the Riviera Casino, jumping naturally enough to the conclusion that he was still under the influence of his systemania. But although I kept him under observation for more than an hour, he did not gamble. Meeting at the bar, we had a drink together, and when I remarked that I hoped he had not invented another system, he laughed. 'No, anyway not yet. You would probably think me a fool if I told you my real reason for being here.'

'Try it,' I said.

'As you already know,' he went on, 'my sense of smell is highly developed. Too highly developed sometimes,' he added wryly, wrinkling his nose and making a gesture which seemed to embrace everyone in the rooms. 'The smell of massed humanity is what may be called the occupational hazard of my trade.'

'And yet,' I interposed, 'one would imagine that people

7

of the kind you meet here are not strangers to soap and water.'

'You are quite right,' he said, 'the people here are reasonably clean. It is not body dirt that troubles me. It is the confusion of odours. You, if your sense of smell is normal, can detect the perfumes of the women and the cigars of the men. But do you notice that there is no distinctive perfume and no distinctive cigar smoke? All the perfumes seem to blend into one perfume, the cigars into one smoke without individuality. That is what makes it so difficult. . . .'

'Makes what so difficult?' I enquired, for I was losing him.

'It is so difficult to classify them.'

'Who in hell wants to classify people by smell?' I wanted to know. 'Surely there are plenty of well-tried and reliable ways? That young woman over there, for example, the one with the fur over her shoulder standing between the tables. You don't need to smell her to know that she's on the make, looking for a soft touch. Then there's that Englishman at the end of the bar. You can tell by listening to him that he's a loud-mouthed shit. Who wants to smell him?'

'I do,' was the quiet reply. 'With civilization we have lost the animals' ability to identify and classify individuals by smell. Watch the quivering of a dog's nostrils as another dog approaches. His nose tells him by methods lost to us whether the other is friend or foe. We are over-civilized. We reach conclusions by a slow process of reasoning, whereas primitive people and animals leap to their conclusions instinctively.'

'Which do you trust?' I asked.

'Instinct, of course,' was the instant reply.

'Mine was a foolish question,' I said. 'Being a Hungarian you would naturally rely on instinct.'

'What has being a Hungarian to do with the matter?' he asked sharply.

'Being a Hungarian, you don't carry the burden of over-civilization.'

He took it very well. 'Although you said it as a joke, you are not far from the truth. You do not have to scratch us very deeply to find the savage. But I must not bore you with my little hobby.'

'Far from being bored, my friend, I am deeply interested. But I confess that I don't altogether grasp your purpose in all this. Why, when there are so many other ways of classifying people, is it important to revive a lost one?'

'Because if that sense was as accurate as I believe it to have been, if I can revive it in myself, I could learn more about you than you know yourself. I will tell you now something that you do not know ... that if you gamble this evening, you will win.'

'What makes you say that?'

'I am not sure. If I knew that I would understand much more than I do at present. If you intend to play, will it annoy you if I watch?'

'Not at all ... provided, of course, that I am a winner.'

At the time when Tisza and I walked over to the nearest roulette table I had in my pocket the sum of, what is now, five hundred new francs. Call it £35. It is the sum I am always willing to lose. In fact, mentally I lose it before playing and anything I have at the end of play ranks as winnings. My approach to the goddess, therefore, is polite but cheerfully indifferent. To lose my stake will not hurt me. It will not be the means of depriving me of anything I want or need. Nor will anyone dependent on me suffer. As I see these things, it means that the goddess and I meet on level terms. I am not important enough for her to want to bring me to my knees, nor arrogant enough to draw her fire. Still less am I stupid enough to suppose that I am entitled to any special consideration at her hands. Seen in precisely this way, gambling ceases to be a vice. The element of folly is minimized to the degree that it becomes an amusement of an innocuous kind. My advice, not that anyone has asked for it, is that if you cannot approach gambling in some such spirit, stay away from it altogether, for it probably means that your make-up lacks the stiffening which only a little iron can give it.

Changing my 500-franc note into chips, I placed a stake

of fifty francs on the numbers 23 and *26 à cheval,* which is to say that if either of them won I would be paid at the rate of 17 to 1. The little ball faltered above the slot of zero, which lies between 26 and 32 on the wheel. Then, after some seconds of hesitation, it dropped neatly into the slot of 26. I had won 850 francs.

Having had a win, my system, if it can be called that, is to put all winnings into my left-hand trouser pocket, not to be touched. The 450 francs left over, after the deduction of the fifty francs stake, went into my right-hand jacket pocket. This and this only was to be used for gambling. The fifty-franc chip already on the table I transferred to the *quatre premiers,* i.e., zero and 1 to 3. Number three won at odds of 8 to 1. Another 400 francs went into the left-hand trouser pocket, making a total of 1,250 francs.

On the next spin I lost my original fifty francs stake, proceeding to lose another 400 francs over the next fifteen minutes, leaving me enough for only one more bet of fifty francs. This I placed on the *sixain* 13 to 18. This won, returning me odds of 5 to 1. Another 250 went into the 'bank'. I left the stake where it was. This, if it lost, was my last bet for the evening, for the *chips* in my trousers pocket were, so to speak, untouchable. The ball dropped into the slot of 16 and another 250 francs was pushed over to me and I still had the fifty francs in hand to play with. For no reason at all I placed this on 29 *en plein,* standing to win 35 times my stake. 'You must tell me the secret,' I said laughingly to János Tisza as the ball dropped into the slot of 29 like a homing pigeon. I pocketed 1,750 francs and let the fifty francs lie. Zero won the next spin, and having no further interest in the play, I led my companion back to the bar. I had won 3,500 francs less my original 500, a net win 3,000 francs, or £210.

Grasse perfumers are not noted for their generosity so, János Tisza being half my age, I permitted myself the liberty of offering him some of my winnings.

'No, please, I prefer not. It is I who am grateful to you for you have helped me to confirm my theory.'

As he did not say anything more about the theory, I let him leave in time to catch the last bus back to Grasse. I would have offered to drive him back but for the somewhat smug cat-that-found-the-cream expression he wore.

It might be argued that I should have felt grateful to the young Hungarian, which is childish nonsense unless it is contended that he had in some mysterious fashion beyond my ken influenced the little ivory ball in its gyrations. Since I declined to believe any such poppycock, it followed that I owed him no debt of gratitude, or of any other kind, unless I were mug enough to believe that had things gone the other way, he would have participated in my losses.

While drinking a solitary brandy and soda I espied coming in my direction my friend Monsieur Chartrain who, in point of strict accuracy, cannot be called a friend. He is a director of the Riviera Casino where behind the scenes I have been told he wields great power. We have known each other on terms of mutual esteem for many years. He is an urbane little man whom it is always a pleasure to meet. He is also, I should add, a purposeful man, which gave me to wonder what was on his mind. I had not long to wait.

'*Sans indiscretion,*' he began, 'might I enquire how well you know Monsieur Tisza?'

'I cannot claim to know him very well,' I replied, 'and the little I know is not unfavourable. We have a mutual friend, a Hungarian, who introduced us in Paris some time ago. Now, I understand, he is a *nez* at the Parfumerie Morel in Grasse. Equally, *sans indiscretion,* may I enquire the nature of your interest in him?'

'Monsieur Tisza is a mystery, *entre nous,* and we of the casino do not like mysteries. This young Hungarian comes here five evenings out of seven. He has never been seen to play. He never speaks to anyone . . . you are the first. . . .'

'Then am I to assume that he is under surveillance?' I asked.

'Surveillance is rather too strong a word,' replied Chartrain. 'He interests me and members of the staff have instructions, if anything unusual occurs, to report the matter to me. This evening it was reported to me that you and he were in conversation so, knowing that we can count on each other's discretion, I sought you out.'

This was so transparently truthful that I stifled any feeling of annoyance I had.

'It may interest you to know,' I said, 'that Tisza has the reputation of being a brilliant mathematician, but of that I am no judge. On the evening I first met him he was trying to promote a syndicate of compatriots to finance a new roulette system of his own invention.'

'I am so pleased you have told me this, *mon cher,* for it may be that the young man is in process of evolving another system. The first one failed, doubtless?'

'Naturally,' I replied.

'Be assured, my friend,' said Chartrain with an evil grin, 'that from this minute any kind of surveillance will cease. Monsieur Tisza is an honoured guest and I will see that for the future he is treated as such. I doubt whether we would have survived the stormy years had it not been for the splendid help of the system players. Do you happen to know the nature of the new system?'

'No, I fear I cannot satisfy you on the point, but I suspect that it has something to do with the stars. He persuaded me to play this evening by assuring me that I would win. Furthermore, I did win. . . .'

'Indeed, yes. Something in the nature of three thousand francs, was it not?'

'So *I* am under surveillance, too?'

'Only indirectly and in so far as we were keeping an eye on your companion. But since we are on the subject, I will confess that we regard your system of one-way traffic into your trousers pocket with the darkest suspicion. Supposing everyone adopted it, how would we live?'

This encounter had been on a plane of light badinage, but I detected an underlying seriousness in our exchange.

On the drive home I was inclined to take János Tisza far more at his own valuation than at any time previously. He was on to something, of that I felt sure. He had the amazing versatility of his race, coupled with a tenacity of purpose which I found somewhat frightening. I try always to remember that in a predominantly Western, or Anglo-Saxon, world it must be very difficult to be a Hungarian. If they appear to us to be an odd lot, it is because that is precisely what they are, especially those who were adults when they left Hungary. Language alone creates for them a tremendous barrier, while mere survival is a notable feat. János Tisza had some deep purpose which was not apparent to the naked eye.

Some such thoughts must have been in the mind of Pierre Morel, for when at our next meeting I enquired about the doings of his Hungarian *nez*, he said: 'It is quite uncanny how he has taken to our life. Except for his accent, he might well be a Grassois, born and bred in the perfume industry, and yet, contradictory though it may sound, I cannot escape the feeling that his true interests are elsewhere. There is a faraway look in his eyes sometimes which suggests that his thoughts are on some remote and distant horizon.'

'Do you suspect him of planning to steal your secrets? Of wanting to take them back to Hungary to start a perfume industry there?'

'We have no secrets. Our stock-in-trade is experience, long experience, which is something which cannot be stolen or bartered. The only secrets, if there are any, are carried in that sharp nose of his. You and I see beauty through the eyes. Our ears bring us lovely sounds. But not János Tisza. The only beauty which exists for him is perceived by way of his nose. He functions through his nose. For all practical purposes he is tone-deaf and colour-blind.'

I can only account for my preoccupation with János Tisza and his strange behaviour by confessing that I have always been inordinately interested in the abstruse. I might have liked the man if there had been anything there to like. He neither gave off nor attracted warmth. He did not offer or ask for friendship. His goal, whatever it was, had little to do with human beings. Yet he made me feel that he regretted the fact that there was no room in his life for friendship.

On my next visit to the Riviera Casino, after the lapse of six or seven weeks, I learned from Chartrain that Tisza had been a constant visitor, but that he had changed his habits. Instead of coming in the early evening, he was in the habit of arriving at about 10 p.m. and staying until shortly after midnight. I left early that evening, so I did not see him.

Our next encounter was late one evening after I had been dining with a party at the casino restaurant. I don't think he saw me at first. He was standing at a shemmy table, as close as the railing would permit, behind a strikingly beautiful young woman who was gambling heavily without much success. She wore a gown of pale blue trimmed, if that is the word, with chocolate brown. I seem to remember a diagonal sash over one shoulder and a band round the waist of the same colour. She had warm brown hair which was a good match for the sash.

So, Tisza is human after all, was my private reflection, seeing his intense concentration on her. But what puzzled me was that when she won he frowned almost as though he hoped she would lose. Her bank ran four or five times and there was a considerable sum in it, around two thousand francs.

I saw the skin tighten across Tisza's prominent cheekbones. His colourless eyes glinted. 'Banco!' he called softly.

Looks of astonishment appeared on several faces, making it quite evident that, known as a man who never gambled, he had succumbed to the temptation at last. Holding a court card and a nine, Tisza was the winner. Pocketing his winnings, he walked across to a roulette table without even glancing at the young woman who had lost the bank.

We met a little later at the bar where, I noticed, he drank a mineral water. 'I dare not drink alcohol,' he told me by way of explanation. 'It blunts the sense of smell. Being a Hungarian, I like highly spiced food, but it is not for me,' he added sadly.

14

'That was a beautiful young woman who lost her bank to you,' I remarked.

'Was she?' he said. 'I am afraid I did not notice.'

'You appeared to be enormously interested in her.'

'I was, but for reasons which had nothing to do with her beauty. She is a person who should not gamble. If I knew her I would tell her so. . . .'

'Is that what made you decide to play this evening?'

'But of course. As she was going to lose anyway, I thought I might as well win it before somebody else did.'

'You sound as if you were very sure of your ground,' I said.

'Yes, quite sure,' he said calmly. 'You see, she was desperate, so she was bound to lose.'

'I don't believe that you were anything like as sure as you pretend to have been.'

'I cannot make you believe if you do not wish to,' he said in the same unflustered way, 'but perhaps it will help you to believe when I tell you that I called "Banco!" with only about twenty francs in my pocket. That is how certain I was.'

'Whether you know it, or not,' I said coldly, 'what you did was a criminal offence. You could have gone to gaol for it and, let me add, rightly so. Since we are being frank, or I am, you would be far nearer normal if you had concentrated on that young woman's body rather than her purse.'

'There are more important things in the world than a woman's body,' he said airily.

'Perhaps,' I said, 'but you are too young to think so. What are you? A pansy with an adding machine where his balls ought to be?'

I said a lot more, indeed more than was strictly necessary. I did not in fact believe that he was a pansy, having heard from Pierre Morel that he was by way of being a devil with the girls in the perfumery, and had I believed so I would have long ago dropped him like a hot brick.

When Tisza left the casino, there was a certain coolness

15

between us. What was he made of? There seemed no answer to the question and the more I saw of him the less I understood him. While I am not trying to make a virtue out of preoccupation with sex, any normal young man could not have failed to be tremendously attracted by the voluptuous girl at the shemmy table. Most of the Hungarians I had met had been rams and at sight of her would have been snorting and pawing the ground. What was it, I asked myself, aside from the obvious, which had riveted his attention on her?

Chartrain, pausing at the bar as he made the rounds of the rooms, remarked: 'They tell me that the Hungarian came out of his shell this evening to win a coup. At the table the *chef* was undecided whether, or not, to verify that if he had lost he could have paid. A very delicate decision to have to make, is it not? In his place I think I would have insisted. What would your opinion be?'

'Not being a shemmy player, I have no opinion,' I replied uncomfortably. 'I like the impersonality of the roulette wheel. When I play a card game,' I added, drawing a red-herring across the subject, 'I like to know something about my fellow players.'

'Are you suggesting,' he asked indignantly, 'that we countenance a crooked game?'

'No, far from it, but I do suggest that if there is any crookedness at the shemmy table, it is on the part of the occasional player who escapes your vigilance. I put virtually nothing past the top-flight card manipulators, and while I am sure you do everything you can to thwart them, I am equally sure that a few ... very few, if you like, are too clever for you.'

Chartrain nodded assent rather sadly. 'Interesting as it is, my job tends to destroy my faith in human nature. We are the target for every kind of dishonest trick you could imagine and many more that you could not. On a percentage basis the number of crooks in the world is, I do not doubt, relatively small. But they all come here at one time or another with larceny in their hearts, and if it causes me to take a somewhat cynical view of my fellow men, I must be forgiven.'

Our conversation had been steered away from Tisza, as I intended, although I do not believe that this had escaped Chartrain's acute perceptions. The former, if he hoped to stay clear of trouble, would be well advised to watch his step. I now saw him in a new light as a somewhat desperate character. Furthermore, one with iron nerve. Leaving aside altogether the moral aspects of Tisza's conduct at the shemmy table, it had required sheer nerve and audacity to bet two thousand francs when, if he had lost, he had not the money to cover his loss. He could not have been relying on me to bail him out because he knew perfectly well that I never took more than five hundred francs into the casino. Yet, even as I turned these thoughts over in my head, I recalled that his demeanour had not been that of a man engaged in a desperate venture. Very much the contrary. The impression left on my mind had been that of a man to whom it had not occurred to doubt the outcome of his gamble. This was absurd because the odds as between him and the beautiful girl who held the bank were approximately even. He could not have failed, therefore, to envisage the possibility of her having better cards than he held. Unless ... and I sheered away from the thought ... he really had been as confident as he had appeared to be, and if that were so I had to believe the unbelievable and attribute the whole thing to extra-sensory perception, or something equally improbable.

Until the evening in question I had not been much interested in János Tisza. He had ranked in my mind as just one more peculiar Hungarian. Our meetings had always been fortuitous. Neither had ever sought the other out. But now, curiosity thoroughly whetted, I wanted to see more.

3

As I never go near a casino in summer and spent the early autumn of that year in London, it was nearly six months before I saw or heard anything more of János Tisza and his strange vigil. To me it was and is incredible that a man could spend two or three hours each evening for months in the fevered atmosphere engendered by gambling apparently watching and waiting. And for what? Others, I learned on my return, had been asking the same question without getting an informative reply. Inevitably he had drawn attention to himself.

'There have been several complaints from players who have been disconcerted by his presence. His face, as you will agree,' Chartrain said, 'is expressionless at all times, but it has become more so ... withdrawn is the word. If only he would smile occasionally, he would be tolerable. He is like a man peering into a thick fog, seeing nothing and nobody....'

'Have you done anything about it?' I asked.

'What can I do? He has not conducted himself with any impropriety, or transgressed any of the rules of conduct as laid down for the casino. While the *salle des jeux* is, as its name implies, a place for gambling, gambling is in no way obligatory. Besides, I am now vastly curious. The young man is far from being a fool and only a fool would have wasted so much time without a purpose. He has a purpose, rest assured of that. You tell me that he once invented a mathematical system which, naturally, failed as they are all bound to fail except for those which return a pittance to the old ladies. But whatever plans he has for our discomfiture, you may rule out mathematics as playing any part.'

'You sound as though you are beginning to take him seriously,' I said lightly.

'Yes, despite common sense which tells me I am an imbecile, and a lifetime of experience which tells me that we have nothing to fear from him, or a hundred clever little men like him, I am ashamed to admit that he makes me uneasy. He is welcome to win a few tens of thousands of the casino's money, naturally provided that it is done honestly. It would be a small price to pay if, despite all the probabilities, he really has evolved a system to beat us. If he has, I will be the first to shake his hand and congratulate him ... if. Don't you see, *mon cher*, it is the uncertainty which has unnerved me. A few years ago I would have laughed at the idea but now, perhaps, I am growing old ... losing my touch. Do you suppose that you could speak to him. . . ?'

'No, positively no,' I told him. 'If, despite all the advantages which are on your side, and all the cunningly devised traps you know how to lay, this young man can beat you at your own game ... honestly, he has all my sympathy and admiration. You must do your own dirty work.'

'Yes,' he said wryly, 'I thought you would say something like that.'

November on the Côte d' Azur is the *morte saison*. The hotels are empty, some of them closed altogether to give the staff a rest, while the Riviera Casino is about as cheerful as an undertaker's parlour. Tisza failed to put in an appearance until things became a little livelier in Christmas week. When I next saw him, there was a subtle change. He seemed to have lost some of the look of heavy-lidded introspection he had worn. His faintly saturnine expression had given way to a smile. Shoulders thrown back instead of being hunched forward spoke of confidence. During the ten or fifteen minutes I had him under observation before we met face to face, he appeared to be busy as a bird dog, walking round each of the four roulette tables in turn, pausing here and there, but never for more than half a minute.

János Tisza was looking for something, searching dili-

19

gently. But for what? Or was it someone? At length he paused behind a statuesque middle-aged woman who was not playing. He stood too close, unnecessarily so, it seemed. If she had been an attractive young thing it would have been explicable. But she was a hard-faced, heavy-breathing battleaxe with about as much sex-appeal as a London bus. Her purse, or handbag, which she clutched fiercely, was almost big enough to be called a reticule. After two or three minutes of this, he looked up and saw me, joining me when I sauntered across to the bar. We exchanged the meaningless patter of acquaintances who had not met for some months.

Returning to our muttons, János Tisza positively oozed confidence. 'You seem very pleased with yourself,' I observed.

'Yes, I am most pleased. Tonight I am going to put certain theories to the test and . . . well, we shall see.'

From time to time while we were talking he cast an eye in the direction of the statuesque woman noted previously. She stood there, clutching her bag and watching the table intently. 'She gives me the impression of being desperately anxious to win tonight,' I said.

'How did you know that?' he asked brusquely, barely politely.

'I was visiting casinos before you were born,' I replied none too cordially, 'and strange as it may seem to you, I learned long ago to use my eyes.'

'I am sorry,' said he contritely. 'I did not mean to be rude. It came as a shock to me to find that you too knew her state of mind.'

'How is it you know so much about her state of mind? Is she an old friend?'

'No, I had never seen her in my life until about twenty minutes ago. . . .' Pointedly, he ignored the first of my two questions. Realizing that he had no intention of replying, I did not waste time pressing the matter.

When the woman opened her purse and passed a wad of notes over to be changed into chips, Tisza went over to the table. After a discreet interval I followed.

20

The woman, whom I now thought of as Tisza's guinea-pig, began by betting on the dozens. Whichever dozen she bet on, Tisza bet on the other two. In this way he won five consecutive times. Observing this, she flashed him a look of annoyance and changed her play to the even money chances. When she backed red, he backed black, and vice versa. It was the same with *manque* and *passe* (1 to 18 and 19 to 36) and with *impair* and *pair* (odd and even).

Thus early it was plain that Tisza's system, if it can be called that, was to play against the woman on the assumption that she was a loser. If this assumption were well-founded, it followed that he must win. But, and this was the big question, on what did he base his assumption?

When the woman began to bet on the numbers, Tisza refrained from betting, because if a player bets on a single number, the only way of playing against him would be to bet on the other thirty-six numbers, which would be absurd. Realizing this, the woman continued to play on the single numbers with disastrous effect upon the diminishing roll of banknotes. I have seldom seen such a run of bad luck at the tables. But except for the few early bets before she tumbled to what he was doing, Tisza's winnings were not impressive. Certainly, they did not warrant the preliminary hoo-ha.

Sipping the mineral water he had left at the bar, Tisza showed his disappointment. 'The weak part of my system is that playing against someone soon becomes apparent. Unreasonably, people don't seem to like it. After all, it does not affect them one way or the other . . . does it?'

'When you play against someone,' I said, 'you make it evident that you regard the person in question as a loser. Maybe that is what they don't like. Who wants to be labelled a loser?'

'Yes, I think you are right. Excuse me, but I see a winner at the big table. I will see if I have more success with him.'

He did not give me an opportunity of asking how he identified winners and losers.

When Tisza had taken up a stance alongside a tweed-clad Englishman, who would have looked more at home auctioning pigs at a county fair, I went to the opposite side of the table where I could observe them both.

The Englishman began betting on zero, 26 and 32, the three numbers which adjoin each other on the wheel. Many people do this on the reasonable theory that the man who spins the wheel aims for zero which, generally speaking, benefits the casino more than any other. If the ball misses zero, it might fall into one of the neighbouring slots of 26 and 32. This is predicated on the assumption that roulette is not entirely a game of chance. When I say that I am inclined to agree with this view, I am not imputing any dishonesty on the part of the casinos, certainly not the well-conducted ones, which are the vast majority in France. I am satisfied that, as a relief from sheer boredom, croupiers try to prove to their own satisfaction that there is a tiny element of skill in the game.

Once, many years ago, I tried to relieve the boredom of illness with a roulette wheel beside my bed. Of its kind, made for domestic amusement, it was a good one, although, of course, nothing like as beautifully balanced as those used in casinos. Although I tried for weeks, I was never able to throw a particular number, but by dividing the wheel with chalkmarks into four segments of approximately ninety degrees each, I was able to put the ball into a particular segment a trifle more frequently than pure chance would suggest.

For six spins of the wheel the Englishman and Tisza drew a blank. Tisza lulled the other's suspicions by saying : 'We play the same game, I see.'

On the seventh spin zero came up. The Englishman, with ten francs staked, won 330 francs less the previous losses. Tisza, who had staked twenty francs, won double the sum. Then for the two of them began a phenomenal run of luck. Zero turned up a second time, while 26 and 32 turned up five times in thirteen spins. Each of them in the meanwhile had doubled his stakes so that on each win Tisza raked in 1,320 francs, or near enough £100.

When the Englishman said: 'I think I'll call it a day,'

Tisza agreed that it was time to quit. The Englishman, sensible fellow, cashed in his winnings and left the rooms, presumably to return to his hotel.

I was impressed, but less so than might be imagined, for the vagaries of the roulette wheel, like the tides of fortune itself, are beyond all understanding. It is said that red once turned up twenty-six times consecutively at Monte Carlo. I have been told—I must qualify it that way—that zero, which by rights should turn up once in every thirty-seven spins, failed to appear in over 400 spins. Think what that would do to anyone following zero on an increasing stake!

All that could be said with real certainty was that Tisza and the Englishman had won some money.

Tisza, meanwhile, had transferred his attentions to the far side of the room and was practically nuzzling a woman of indeterminate age who was one of the small group of well-behaved whores permitted to ply their trade in the casino as a service to lonely male visitors. She and her sisters were so discreet that I knew them all by sight for some years without knowing what they were. While I have never subscribed to the whore-with-a-heart-of-gold school, I have a profound sympathy for the unfortunate sisterhood. People will say knowingly that whores are whores because they like it, or because they are too lazy to work, or other facile explanations, some of which may be true. I prefer to believe that along with the men who contract miner's phthisis, lunatics and cripples, life has been unkind to them. However, let that be as it may, the woman in question was at one of the tables where the minimum stake was two francs and was betting *à cheval* on 29–32. Alongside her two-franc stake Tisza dropped fifty francs. Evidently, by whatever route he reached his conclusions, she was a lucky person to follow. Well, without drawing it out, that is exactly what she was. Either 29 or 32 turned up seven times in sixteen spins. The woman won thirty-four francs each time, while Tisza, playing with a fifty-franc stake, won 850 francs. After deducting 450 francs for his losing bets, Tisza won 5,500 francs, or something near £400. This, despite my natural cynicism about such things, I found impressive.

If he had in fact discovered some way of identifying the lucky and the unlucky—and I was still reluctant to believe it—he had the world by the tail.

Before the evening ended I had one more opportunity to put it to the test. Tisza latched on to a well-known Englishwoman who, being the daughter of an earl, was a 'Lady' in her own right. She lost a proverbial packet scattering money all over the board in such a way that Tisza found it impossible to play against her, and when she crossed over to the *trente-et-quarante* table, I followed her. Having been unlucky at roulette, it seemed to me, was no bar to her being unlucky at *trente-et-quarante* also. Here, the odds being even, it was easy to play against her without the fact being apparent. She was betting heavily, while I contented myself with 100-franc stakes. During the ten or twelve minutes before she gave it up in disgust, my net winnings were 800 francs, call it £50.

In degree there is greed and larceny in every heart, with the difference that some keep it under better control than others. I will admit to as much as bars me from being a saint, but not enough to make me dangerous to society, and I would be a fool and a liar to deny that the opening up of that vista of easy money dazzled me. Unless this were just a flash in the pan, which time alone would show, Tisza was on to a very good thing. Two more evenings such as this had been would convince me. I was already halfway convinced, but if the performance I had witnessed could be repeated twice more, then Tisza would appear to have tamed the Goddess of Chance.

Believing that at this juncture a little soft soap would do no harm, I invited the Hungarian to dine with me at the casino restaurant. He accepted with alacrity, giving me the impression that he wanted to say something to me as badly as I wanted to say something to him. I was right.

'Do you think the casino direction have noticed me at all?' he asked.

24

'Not more so than if you came in walking on your hands and wearing silver lamé pyjamas,' I replied. 'They aren't blind, you know. People who come here are supposed to enjoy themselves. For months you behave as though this is the Wailing Wall, looking like a constipated undertaker. Then, suddenly, you begin to look cheerful and win money. Have they noticed you? Not only have they noticed you, my dear fellow, but they know to within ten francs what you have won. Furthermore, they have a written record of every stake you have made, and the bright boys down in the basement will be sitting up all night trying to figure out how it was done. If you go to take a leak their flying squad will search the place for confederates. In short, as from this minute, you are a marked man.'

Tisza looked a little shaken. 'Has anyone questioned you about me?'

'Of course they have ... months ago. In fact, if I hadn't put in a word and said you were harmless, I think you'd have been given the bum's rush. While you lose money, you are welcome as the flowers in May. In fact, the same is true when you win money ... a little money. But establish a regular pattern of winning and you become Public Enemy Number One.'

'What did they ask you?' he wanted to know.

'They wanted to know what you were up to. . . .'

'What did you tell them?'

'The truth, of course, that I didn't know. What else could I have said?'

'Will they question you again, do you think?'

'I don't think ... I know they will, unless of course this table is wired for sound.'

'What will you say?' was the next question.

'That, my clever Hungarian friend, depends on you. If, as seems possible, although highly improbable, you have really stumbled on a goldmine, all you have to do to ensure my complete discretion and co-operation is to cut me in on the good thing. The moment you do that, don't you see, our interests become identical.'

25

'I must think about it,' he said unhappily.

'I imagine,' I said, 'that if this continues to be a money-spinner, you won't be wasting your time in Grasse sniffing perfumes?'

'No, I won't give that up . . . anyway not for a long time.'

As it was already midnight and he had to be at work by 8 a.m., he bade me goodnight and left. He had not been gone more than three minutes when a maître d'hôtel brought me a message from Chartrain to ask if it would be convenient to have him join me for a cup of coffee.

He arrived looking flustered. 'So your young Hungarian friend has declared his hand at last,' he began. 'What can you tell me about it?'

'Nothing, because I know nothing.'

'It is quite apparent that he has a system.'

'Apparent to you,' I hedged, 'but not to me, and if he has a system, I assure you I was not let into the secret.'

'It did not escape notice, my friend, that after Tisza had been unable to profit by Lady X's misfortunes at roulette, you followed her to the *trente-et-quarante* and, by playing against her, won a small sum.'

'Monsieur Chartrain,' I said coldly, 'if I have to submit to interrogation because I happened to win a trifling sum this evening, I fear I shall be compelled to consider amusing myself elsewhere. It would be a pity because in all other respects the management here is admirable.'

'Enjoy your little joke if you will, monsieur, but humour me by answering just one more question. What made you so sure that Lady X would lose and that by playing against her you would win? That is all.'

'To tell you the truth, my friend, is not very gallant, I fear, but the fact is that looking at her horse face convinced me that the lady was unlucky. It followed, therefore, that anyone opposing her would be lucky.'

'I shall be retiring in two years' time,' Chartrain said good-naturedly, 'and I cannot tell you what satisfaction it would give me while I am still here to learn that someone had invented an infallible system of play. I think of the thousands of hours I have wasted over the years trying to analyse the play of individuals in order to determine whether the player relied on a system or plain blind luck. One season before the war a compatriot of yours seriously worried us by winning steadily over a period of seven weeks. He won the equivalent of £80,000 in your money. When he left us he promised to return next year, which he did, and lost it all within the first week he was here. For years now I have laughed at the idea of a system but now ... our young Hungarian friend has raised my doubts again.'

Chartrain wasn't fooling. János Tisza had rattled him. The amount of money involved was negligible. Somebody had to win and be seen to win, for it was that possibility and that alone which brought people to the casino. Sometimes they won large sums. It did not matter so long as the operative factor was chance. But let anyone establish a way of taking the casino's money by any other route than pure chance, the whole structure would be endangered. Remote as he knew the possibility to be, Chartrain would not rest easily in his bed until these doubts had been resolved. If János Tisza had found a loophole in the system, it would be for Chartrain to close it.

*   *   *   *

It was a worried János Tisza who drove to Ste Monique in the new car which he had acquired with the winnings. 'Things are becoming very difficult at the casino,' he told me. 'They watch me as though I were a thief.'

'In their eyes you are a thief,' I reminded him. 'Try losing some money for a change. Then they will love you and maybe call the dogs off. . . .'

'But as soon as I began to win again they would watch me. I was wondering whether you would consider taking my place. . . .'

'What would that achieve? They are aware already that I know you and it would be assumed that you had passed over the system to me. Then both of us would be thrown out of the casino. Anyway, we're wasting time talking non-

27

sense because, as you well know, I don't know what your system is . . . if you have a system.'

'There is no need for you to know my system,' he said calmly. 'Even if I explained it, it would mean nothing to you. In fact, it isn't really a system.'

'When is a system not a system?' I muttered. 'If you don't mind I would rather not talk about it any more until I am satisfied that you really have something. I'll admit it looks as though you have, but it's too soon to jump to conclusions. The casino has jumped to its own conclusion, but I am not ready to yet. It's understandable because it's their money which is at stake, not mine.

'They will let you go on winning money for a time yet, if only because it is the only way they can learn about the system which isn't a system. My advice to you is to go ahead and take their money if you can. Keep your stakes moderately low and, just to throw them off the scent, lose occasionally. Then, if you're lucky, it will be some weeks before they withdraw your admission card.'

In French resorts where there are casinos it is an unwritten rule, and a very good one, that people directly concerned with the running of a casino do not in any circumstances whatever make any sign of recognition when meeting casino clients elsewhere. Many people, for their own good reasons, do not wish to be known as casino habitués. I was astounded, therefore, when drinking a solitary apéritif in the sunshine, to hear Chartrain's muttered apology as he took the vacant chair at my table. 'Did you hear what happened last evening?' he asked excitedly. I shook my head. 'Our young Hungarian friend won over sixty thousand francs.'

This being more than four thousand pounds, was too much to be dismissed as a trifle.

'Well, there's plenty more where that came from,' I remarked indifferently.

Chartrain looked shocked. In what are called the upper financial brackets in France, and for that matter in most countries, it is not considered correct, or polite, to be flippant

28

about money. It ranks with smoking a cigar without removing the band, wearing a made-up bow tie and poisoning foxes. It is just not done and I think the slight coolness which developed between us from that moment is attributable far more to my flippancy than to the fact that I appeared to be on friendly terms with a young man who had taken a substantial sum of money from the casino by unorthodox means.

'Tonight, if he presents himself at the door, he will be refused admission.'

'So you kiss the sixty thousand francs goodbye. . . .'

'Yes, although I am not altogether sure that it is the wise thing to do. I think perhaps we are being premature, but my co-directors think otherwise.'

I was more understanding of Chartrain's viewpoint than I appeared to be. The complex, smooth-working machinery of the Riviera Casino was geared to the simple fact that whatever happened to the individual players, win or lose, a percentage of the total turnover must stick to the casino. There were good days and bad days, of course, but in the long run the percentage remained a constant. Now, confronted by the bare possibility that an ingenious brain had evolved a way of upsetting this desirable outcome, Chartrain and his co-directors had been thrown off balance and were experiencing panic. Or so it seemed.

If this quiet, unassuming young Hungarian had, against all the probabilities, stumbled on the Infallible System, every gambling establishment in the world was threatened. When Tisza had won all the money he wanted—if there is ever a limit to human greed—there was nothing to prevent him passing his knowledge over to others.

Quite suddenly it dawned upon me that this knowledge, or method, or system, whatever it might be, was too dangerous to be desirable. I did not want it to be supposed that I was privy to it.

Although it had been my intention to return home early that evening, I decided to go to the casino instead. I would play with my usual 500 francs and in the manner I had always played before knowing Tisza. I enjoyed my harmless little gambles too much to want to be associated with him and, as would inevitably happen, have my admission card withdrawn.

I was in an unhappy frame of mind when I reached the casino at about seven o'clock that evening. I was not in the mood to gamble and resented what I felt was the necessity to do so.

Wandering across to the 'big' roulette table, it was not long before I became aware of being under surveillance. The same three men appeared as I went from table to table. It wasn't very cleverly done, which meant that I was intended to know it as a delicate hint that if I played any monkey tricks I would be sure to be spotted. However foolish it may sound in its context, I did not care whether I won or lost. Out of temper, I wanted to cut it short.

Pausing at the *trente-et-quarante* table, the only one in play at that time, I put my 500-franc note on red. Red won. Leaving 500 on red, I put the other 500 on *couleur*. *Rouge* and *couleur* won. My 500 francs had become 2,000. I played the same game with doubled stakes. There was not a lot of money on the table so mine was conspicuous. I had 4,000 francs. This, on the spur of the moment, I transferred to black. Black won. Picking up my winnings, with the escort in attendance, I went across to a roulette table where zero had just been the winning number. While one spin of the wheel cannot influence another, I would never in ordinary circumstances dream of backing a number which had just won. Nevertheless, I put 100 francs on zero. Zero won and 3,500 francs were pushed across to me.

Even if I could remember the details, I feel that my word would be doubted if I were to recite the events of the next hour. Let it suffice to say that I won more than I have ever won, before or since, at a casino. In my effort to dissociate myself from János Tisza, I had made it seem highly probable that he and I were in cahoots and that I was privy to his system.

30

As I made for the bar, my escort disappeared, presumably to report.

'You played like a man who did not care whether he won or lost, I am told,' said Chartrain when he passed the bar, 'but in case the thought is in your mind, nobody who saw you could be so foolish as to believe that yours was anything but sheer blind luck.'

This happened to be true, but I had not credited him with being so perceptive.

I was pleased rather than otherwise when János Tisza failed to get in touch with me during the weeks which followed. The next news I had of him was from Pierre Morel, who told me that he had quit his job at the perfumery and, so far as anyone knew, vanished. 'I feel very much annoyed,' Morel told me, 'because he left without notice with some important work unfinished. I deserved better at his hands, for he had been treated generously. In fact, if this had not happened, I was contemplating giving him a share in the business. He and my daughter, it seems, had some kind of an understanding, because she has been most unhappy since he left.'

That, or so I thought, was that.

4

As my loyal band of readers knows and has known for many years, my adopted home is the former Provençal fishing village of Ste Monique. I say former because nobody there now troubles to fish. There is far more to be made, with far less expenditure of sweat, by swindling tourists. Although I have been heard to deplore the decline of Ste Monique, I doubt really whether its decline has been on a greater scale than anywhere else. London for instance, where the hairy pansy yobbos appear to be firmly in the saddle.

One of the reasons, if not the only one, why I did not pull up stakes years ago is that to have done so would have meant parting from my old friend Father Delorme, who has the village cure of souls. Not mine, of course, because, if he is to be believed, mine is beyond redemption. On such matters, our affection being mutual, we agree to disagree. He disagrees with me violently because he cannot afford to have it said that he shares my heretical views. I frequently pretend to disagree with him, when in fact I am in full agreement, because I know that opposition is good for him. The cloying mock-humility of his flock is what threatens to destroy him.

On my return from the successful assault upon the Riviera Casino, I happened to mention the fact to the old priest who, smelling money, tried to separate me from some. The appeal was on behalf of the church bell which had cracked again a bare ten years after he had hornswoggled me into paying for it to be recast.

'Once in a lifetime is enough for anyone. Let the people who live nearer than I do to it pay for it. A little cotton wool in my ears on Sunday mornings is all I need, and then only when there is a mistral blowing from the West. . . .'

'You carry your selfishness to extreme limits,' he growled.

'But not as far as you do,' I was forced to tell him. 'There are far more people annoyed by the church bell than pleased by it. I consider it an affront at a time when there is a national campaign, sponsored in the highest quarters in the land, to reduce noise. Motorists, even taxi-drivers, have cut down noise to the minimum. Would you have it said that they are more public-spirited than the Church?'

If there was a flaw in my argument, I have failed to find it just as he failed to point it out. He denounced me in unspecific terms, making almost as much noise as the bell in the process. With a change in the topic of conversation, his decibel output dropped and we were able to chat like civilized people.

The next thing I heard was that there was to be a Tombola, or raffle, in aid of the project. For the sake of peace and quiet I bought a ticket. In life one submits to a lot of mild blackmail for the sake of peace and quiet.

One morning soon after my return I went for an apéritif to Lentrua's bar, which is the social centre of Ste Monique. Sitting on a stool, the only customer in the place, was János Tisza, drinking the eternal mineral water without much enthusiasm. I think I mentioned elsewhere that he had friends in Ste Monique, people whom I knew only by repute. 'I imagined you a long way away,' I said, 'having a triumphant tour of Europe, leaving a trail of bankrupt casinos behind you. Something gone wrong?'

'Yes, very wrong,' was the lugubrious reply. 'I've been barred from every casino on the coast.'

'Winning too much money, is that it?'

'I didn't win much, except for that one evening at the Riviera Casino. What made them suspicious of me was that I won every time I went and ... well, they didn't seem to like it.'

'I'm not surprised. Now what are you going to do?'

'I think I shall go up to Aix-les-Bains and Divonne.'

'Don't waste your time,' I told him. 'If you are blacklisted on the coast, you are blacklisted everywhere in France by now, and possibly elsewhere. The casinos have, or used to have, a kind of central clearing house for information. Anyone who caused trouble, issued stumer cheques, or was suspected of any kind of dirty work in any casino in Europe, had a dossier which was available to any member casino. I think you can be sure it exists today in some form or other. The headquarters, I was once told, was in Brussels.'

'I shall have to think about it,' he said. 'May I come to talk it over with you one day soon?'

'Why not?'

We left it at that.

Shortly after this János Tisza and his troubles were driven out of mind by a phone call from Esmé, the daughter of my old friend Broom* who, when standing on his dignity, liked to be known more correctly as Eduardo Jaime St Firmin Plantagenet y Alvarado.

Since the death of her father I have tried, without much success, to take his place in her life. Like her father, Esmé tends to be rather wild at times.

Her news was bad. She and her husband, a young Scot named Latta, whom I had liked, had come to the parting of the ways. I didn't listen to the reasons because in my experience one never hears the whole truth about husband and wife brawls, partly because the reasons become obscured by the facts. There are, for all practical purposes, only three reasons: another woman, another man, or money. Incompatibility is usually a long word to cover one of these.

I learned long ago never to listen to these recitals of woe, taking a leaf from the book of a psycho-analyst in whose company I once travelled by train from Montreal to Vancouver. He was a very successful practitioner, owing much of his success to the fact that he was nearly stone deaf. He would listen to his patients for the first few minutes while they got into their stride so to speak. Then he would switch off his hearing aid and go into a trance. When his secretary rang through to say that the next customer was waiting, he would tell the patient to reduce her story to

* *Broom*, by Stephen Lister, Peter Davies Ltd, 1969.

writing—sometimes it was *his* story—and bring it at the next consultation. There is as much virtue in appearing to listen as in listening. The patient wants to spill the dirt, get it out of his system. On the same principle boils are lanced.

Esmé's phone call was from New York, and two days later I was waiting for her plane to put down at Nice airport, where it was a mere seven hours late.

The arrival of a lovely young woman in a bachelor establishment like mine might have caused some little awkwardness. But not in the case of Esmé, who had stayed with me before without a chaperon.* Esmé's attitude to the conventions was to ignore them. It may have been hereditary, for her father had been like that. So, if it did not trouble her, I could afford to shrug off the inevitable eyebrow lifting in the small community of Ste Monique.

Esmé's tale of woe, whose essential details could have been told in five minutes while sipping a cool drink, required seven hours for the first instalment and the best part of two more days for the balance. Shorn of all unnecessary verbiage and histrionics, only one real fact emerged: her marriage was on the rocks and was likely to remain there. I was sympathetic because I was, and am, very fond of the girl and hated to see her looking so unhappy. The rest signified as much as a pink paper frill on a ham.

One more broken marriage. Whose fault was it? Obviously, they shared the blame. What else in all conscience was there to say? Having let her blow off steam to her heart's content, I had done my duty. 'Until you have come to some definite decision about the future,' I told her firmly, 'let us regard the subject as closed.'

'But I need your advice,' she wailed.

'You don't. Even if I were fool enough to give it to you, you wouldn't follow it.'

'You bastard!'

*   *   *   *

* Readers under forty years af age, who may never have heard this word, should consult a dictionary.

35

Alphonsine, who has looked after my creature comforts these many years, had been devoted to my old friend Broom. Women of all ages and social strata fell under the spell of his splendid good looks and an arrogance softened by impeccable good manners. This had caused a certain friction in my household, for while I want my guests to be comfortable, I refuse to be neglected to that end and to sit back gnashing my teeth while they wallow in luxury.

A small household like mine cannot cope with guests who demand special attention. 'I make the rules here,' I told Esmé firmly. Realizing that I meant what I said, she radiated sweetness and light.

Esmé had some little peculiarities and one of them had far-reaching consequences ... for her. On a brilliant summer's morning János Tisza phoned to say that if convenient he would like to see me about something. I forget what. I suggested that he come to lunch. Taking a short cut often used by people who came on foot, the way led him past the guest bungalow, outside which Esmé was taking a sun-bath stark naked. Without professing to be an authority on the subject, I would say that the average—there is no such thing, of course—gently nurtured young woman would have proceeded to cover herself or, if possible, taken some evasive action such as diving for cover.

Esmé did neither. János goggled. 'If you've seen enough, bugger off!' said the recumbent Esmé calmly.

When these two met at the luncheon table they did so as strangers and it was not until some time later that I learned of the encounter.

One reads of sparks kindled by the meeting of two kindred souls, although I am persuaded that the phenomenon is rarer than indicated in the pages of fiction. Well, it happened at my dining-table right under my eyes. Esmé was the catalyst. She did not seem to change, but János underwent a complete transformation. The quiet, introspective, somewhat scholarly young Hungarian seemed to shed all his inhibitions in the sunshine of Esmé's smiles.

The longer I live the more reluctant I am to introduce

people to each other, especially when I sense the explosive possibilities of the meeting. In the case of these two I could see no likelihood of an affinity, basing my belief on the fact that János was a Hungarian and, therefore, partly Turk and, going back a little further, partly Mongol-Tartar. Like every Hungarian I have ever met, he had an Oriental attitude towards women. Esmé being what she was—undisciplined, violent-tempered and fearlessly outspoken— would be altogether lacking in the qualities demanded of a Hungarian harem woman. I wished him joy of trying to tame her.

For the next few days Esmé did as I like my guests to do: she treated the house as an hotel, coming and going just as she pleased and having the courtesy to let Alphonsine know whether or not she would be in for a meal. I abominate the kind of guest who intrudes on my breakfast by asking: What are we going to do today?

It was nearly a week before I had the opportunity of a *tête-à-tête* with Esmé who, I suspect, was beginning to think she was neglecting me.

'Is János as clever as he appears to be?' she asked, coming straight to the point over Sunday evening's cold meal.

'I wouldn't be surprised if he is cleverer even than he looks. It's only in the matter of human relations that I've found him a trifle green. I don't think he understands people.'

'Do you like him?'

'Yes, moderately,' I replied. 'He isn't easy to know.'

'Do you trust him?'

'If by that you mean would I trust him in all matters and circumstances, the answer is no. But in many ways I would be inclined to. I don't think you realize how little I know him. Anyway, why do you ask?'

'That's a bloody silly question,' she snapped.

'Yours is a bloody rude answer,' I retorted.

'Yes, I suppose it was,' she said, making it sound like a half-hearted apology. 'To come down to facts and cases,' she went on, 'if I were your daughter, would you trust him with me?'

'No, I don't think I would. Equally, if he were my son, I'd ship him off to Australia before I'd let him marry you.'

That seemed to amuse her, for she roared with laughter.

My relationship with Esmé—her baptismal name was Esmeralda—is not an easy one to define. Indeed, it may be said not to exist at all. It rests on the simple facts that, despite everything, I like her, and that her father, just such another 'difficult' character, was a schoolfriend. No, there is a third. Admitting one evening to a premonition that he would not make old bones, he asked me to keep an eye on her. With a gulf of more than forty years between us, and lacking any kind of authority, there was little, short of equipping her with a chastity belt, that I could do about her sex life.

Esmé insisted that her break with Latta, the Scots engineer she had married, was irreparable. But this I doubted. If it were so, I believed, she would not talk about him so much. When one writes people off one does not talk about them. I liked the little I had seen of Latta, who was quiet, sober-minded, the kind of man, without much brilliance, who would plod steadily to his goal. He was, in short, every-thing that she was not. Instead of singing his praises, which would have driven them further apart, I repeated some of the things which Esmé herself had said about him. Among these were such gems as 'selfish bastard', 'bloody prig' and 'self-satisfied Scotch sod'. When she flew to his defence, I felt I knew all I needed to know. Thereafter I remained strictly neutral, hoping that the breach would be healed.

In the meanwhile, János had arrived on the scene to complicate matters. Inevitably, my feelings about him were coloured by the episode at the shemmy table when he had called 'Banco!' with effectively nothing in his pocket. It was, of course, downright crooked, but essentially less crooked than many practices which we condone. Windbag politicians, who will promise anything before elections, without the smallest intention of being true to their pledges, are still referred to in the House of Commons as 'the Honourable Member'. The worst punishment they ever receive is to be rejected by their constituents next time in favour of another crook. János had at least taken a big risk and had required an iron nerve to carry it through. In the matter of honesty there was nothing to choose between him and the politician. There remained the obstacle that Esmé was already married, but I doubted whether, despite being a Roman Catholic, she would allow it to stand between her and something she desired.

Not long after this, Esmé buttonholed me one evening and without any preliminary circumlocution, for which I liked her, launched into the subject uppermost in her mind. 'What do you know about the infallible gambling system which János claims to have invented?'

'I really *know* nothing,' I told her, 'except that he appears to have won some money and that on his advice I won a little.'

'Is it crooked, do you think?' she asked. 'I don't care if it is, but I'd like to know. I'm like Father in that. I'd rather be honest than dishonest, but if I'm going to do something dishonest, I want to go into it with my eyes open. A man once tried to seduce me, but I didn't give him the chance ... I seduced him. That way, don't you see, I didn't feel so cheap and he couldn't boast of it.'

'Let's stick to roulette systems,' I said, 'and for the future please try not to talk to me as though I were your Mother Confessor. I'm not as old as all that and it isn't flattering. As to whether the system is crooked, or not, I just haven't formed an opinion. I don't even know what the system is ... if there is a system. Anyway, what's your interest in the matter?'

'János wants me to operate it for him. . . .'

'Then surely he's the man to ask about it. . . ?'

'I have asked him,' Esmé replied. 'But he says that even if he told me about it, I wouldn't believe him. He says, and it makes sense, that I should see it in operation before passing judgment. What he tells me is that he has discovered a way of sorting out lucky and unlucky players in advance of play, so that by following the lucky ones and playing against the unlucky ones, you win.'

'As far as it goes, I know that much,' I told her, 'and to be fair I have to admit that I saw him win a little, and a friend of mine who is a director of the Riviera Casino tells me he won about 60,000 francs one evening.'

'And because of it, he tells me,' said she in high indignation, 'they've put the bar up against him.'

'They think he's got something,' I told her, 'and they just hate losing money. They're funny that way.'

'Then if they really think he's got something,' she said, 'it's good enough for me.'

'But how will you be able to work it if János isn't allowed into the casinos on the coast and perhaps elsewhere?'

'János says he can pick the winners and the losers *before* they go into the casino. He'll point them out to me. I follow them in and Bob's your uncle. Do you think it's all right for me to go in with him?'

'Listen, my dear girl. You'll get no advice from me on that subject, not that you'd take it if I gave you any. It's something you must decide for yourself. Then, if something goes wrong, you'll only have yourself to blame.'

'Do you think something will go wrong?'

'Esmé, my dear, János is a Hungarian and where Hungarians are concerned anything can happen, anything from the best to the worst. You could end up so rich that instead of parking your Rolls-Royces you just abandon them. Equally, you could end up in gaol. That's the glorious uncertainty of associating with Hungarians. It isn't a case of honesty or dishonesty. It's just that they never seem to do anything as other people do. . . .'

'I know one exception to that,' said Esmé, making it sound better by blushing.

So it was like that.

Progress was slowed because Esmé had never played roulette and did not understand even the rudiments of the game. I had a roulette wheel and the green baize board which I used to bring out occasionally for the amusement of guests, so János and I initiated her into its childishly simply mysteries. When we considered that she knew enough, János taught her a sort of code for pointing out the lucky or the unlucky.

Alongside the Riviera Casino was the Baccara Bar, much frequented by gamblers because the price of drinks was less than half the exorbitant prices in the casino itself.

As neither of them had a car—János had smashed his up—I drove them, parking the car some four hundred yards from the casino. It was advisable for me not to be seen with either of them and for them not to appear to be together. All three of us went independently to the Baccara, where I took a stool at the bar, while they each occupied a small table. At a near-by table was a Corsican I knew by sight and reputation, one of the heaviest gamblers on the coast. From his conversation with people at another table it was apparent that he was drinking an apéritif before playing. I had seen him win eighteen millions of old francs at a session and lose nearly as much at another, so he could not be classified as either a lucky or unlucky player. 'I am not interested in people who are generally lucky, or unlucky,' János had explained. 'That wouldn't help us because generally lucky people can be unlucky on a particular day, or the other way round. The whole basis of my system is that I must know whether someone is going to win or lose at a particular time.'

'What you're saying in effect,' I said somewhat sourly, 'is you have an infallible system for betting on horses by knowing in advance which horse is going to win.'

The Corsican's 'system', if it can be called that, was to bet on two dozens and to treble his stakes when he lost up to a maximum of three losing spins. If this were going to be one of his losing nights it would be easy to play against him by betting on the other dozen. When Esmé went into the casino alone soon after the Corsican went, I could not tell whether János had tipped him as a winner or a loser, but it soon became apparent when I saw him and Esmé at the same table that she was betting against him.

41

To avoid any association with Esmé, I played in exactly the same way as she did, always against the Corsican. To make it appear that I was one of the idiots who play at two tables simultaneously, I bet on an occasional number at another table. When he had lost somewhere around the equivalent of £6,000 I, playing with much smaller stakes, had won the equivalent of £400, which was for me a large sum.

When the Corsican gave up in disgust, I went to the bar where I had not long to wait before Chartrain stopped on his round. 'You seem to have abandoned your usual style of play,' he remarked amiably enough.

'Creatures which are predictable,' I said, 'don't last long in the jungle.'

For fifteen or twenty minutes I did not see Esmé, so I assumed she had rejoined János at the Baccara. When she reappeared she was trailing, and none too cleverly, an elderly woman whom I knew by sight but not by name. I had always thought her to be English, but I heard her speaking Dutch to a compatriot. One does not see many Hollanders gambling. Where possible Esmé played against her, evidence that János had tipped her as a loser. I did likewise, with the result that my earlier winnings began to melt. Meanwhile, flushed with success, the Dutchwoman increased her stakes and at the end of some thirty or forty minutes had a huge pile of chips in front of her. I gave up when all my winnings had vanished and I had lost my original 500 francs stake. It had seemed the night for breaking my own rule and playing with my winnings.

The loss of my winnings was salutary, for if I had continued to win, I reflected, I might have been tempted to believe that János really had stumbled on a way of beating the roulette wheel. This in turn could have led me into incalculable follies.

Esmé must have lost plenty. How much I could not guess, for I had studiously avoided showing any interest in her. I watched her as she walked dejectedly out of the rooms, glad for her sake that she was a loser. With far less experience of gambling than I had, she might easily have fallen into the error of supposing that it was easy to win.

Alone with my thoughts, this was a good moment to re-assess the János system. The events of the evening had not entirely shattered my faith in it, for all I had learned in essence was that it was fallible and only a fool would have believed otherwise. My experience tells me that the most dangerous moment in gambling comes when one believes oneself to be clever.

On the way out of the rooms. I paused at the table where the Dutchwoman was still playing. Her huge pile of chips had gone and she was digging into her purse for fresh wads of notes.

Esmé and János appeared sunk deeply in gloom when I returned to the Baccara, the latter especially so. 'I do not understand,' he was saying, 'for I was certain that she would lose.'

I said nothing until, after collecting the car, we were well on the way back to Ste Monique. 'It may interest you both to know,' I said, 'that almost immediately after Esmé left the rooms the woman began to lose. When I left all her winnings had gone and she was playing with her own money again. Your timing was bad, that's all. . . .'

'You are probably right,' said János, 'but my method does not take into account that a player may be a good winner and a bad loser all within an hour.'

'And yet,' I pointed out, 'that is the usual pattern. You do not often see unbroken good or bad luck for any length of time.'

5

As always when he came up against facets of life with which
he was unfamiliar, Father Delorme had a healthy curiosity.
Where János and his system were concerned, the old priest
seemed interested to the point of fascination. 'What you
tell me is, in effect,' he said, 'that this young Hungarian, by
means at present unknown to you, is able to anticipate the
vagaries of Chance. Am I right?'

'Roughly so, yes,' I replied.

'I find it incredible,' he said.

'So do I,' I told him, 'despite the fact that at his direction
I have won gratifying sums of money, and I assure you I
have no better idea than you do of how it is done.'

'Then, if you accept the proposition that no man can do
the impossible, it is quite evident that somewhere in it there
is trickery.'

'Depending upon how you define trickery, Father, you
may well be right. But let me tell you that the men who
control gambling casinos are not easily tricked. Once, perhaps, but let them smell trickery and be forewarned, they
will get to the root of the matter. Those people are up to
more tricks than even a priest. . . .'

Ordinarily, that would have drawn his fire, but he let it
pass. 'It is quite absurd,' he said.

'You regard it as absurd and, for purposes of this discussion, so do I. But the directors of the casinos along the
coast do not share our view. They regard it as such a
dangerous threat to their existence that they have put up the
bar against him.'

'That persuades me to take the young man more seriously,'
said Father Delorme, lips pursed and brow furrowed with
perplexity. 'Never having gambled in my life,' he went on,

'the mysteries of Chance have always fascinated me. If, as I and any good Christian must believe, God is omniscient, omnipotent and omnipresent, a leaf or a raindrop cannot fall without his knowledge and consent. From that point one must go further to enquire whether, since a falling leaf is worthy of God's notice, the movement of the little ivory ball round the roulette wheel is not also. . . .'

There was, of course, a lot more, because it is not in the nature of a priest to dismiss God with a hundred words when a thousand would sound more impressive. But I do not deny that if one accepts the falling leaf analogy one must accept the hand of God at the roulette table, if for no other reason than that human lives are frequently influenced profoundly thereby. Nevertheless, I found the water too deep for a simple chap like me.

*　　　*　　　*　　　*

It was some time later when it occurred to me that I had not visited Father Delorme recently so, on the spur of the moment, I decided to go to see him. I was half way to the garage when I heard the strident ringing of the phone. Lifting the receiver, I heard to my astonishment the voice of the old priest himself. I say to my astonishment because I had never known him for any reason whatsoever to use the telephone, an instrument he disliked and refused to have in his house. With a needless decibel output, he told me that he wanted to talk to me. When I said that I had already been on my way to see him, the crash as he replaced the receiver nearly deafened me.

'Why,' he greeted me, 'did you not tell me that our Hungarian friend was a *nez* in a Grasse perfumery?'

'Because I attached no importance to it,' I replied. 'In any case, he is no longer a *nez*. If I had known you were summoning me on such a trivial errand, I would have stayed at home.'

'Would you still call the matter trivial if I told you that I had solved the mystery of your Hungarian friend's roulette system?'

'If you have—I repeat, if you have—solved it, no I would not consider it trivial,' I replied. 'Have you?'

'I regard it as quite possible that I have done so, but before we discuss the matter any further, I must ask you to spare me your witticisms, at least until I have finished telling you the nature of my conclusions.'

There was, I need hardly add, a great deal of circumlocution before he got around to an exposition of his amazing theory.

'You may believe me, or not, as your sceptical mind dictates,' he began, 'that a man who has a true vocation for the priesthood learns much about his fellow men. One of his first problems is to distinguish between the sincere and insincere. Some never succeed in doing so and, if themselves sincere, are to be pitied. This, I am persuaded, is instinctive rather than acquired knowledge, and its possession smooths many paths.

'You must accept as the fact it is,' he went on, 'that my instinct in this matter seldom betrays me. True penitence ranks as sincerity, while mock penitence is an abomination, often worse than the sin which precedes it. As many as fifty years ago, amazed even then by the accuracy of this instinct, I began to enquire into its nature. The answer came to me one day when a woman, a stranger passing through the village, came to confess. I knew as she entered the confessional, before she opened her mouth to speak, that she was a mock penitent. My nostrils twitched and my anger rose. "Woman," I said, "it were better that you remain unconfessed than that you come here prepared to lie to God, beside which your other sins are nothing." She began to weep bitterly. Sending her away, I told her that I would see her an hour thence, urging her not to return unless there were true penitence in her heart. . . .'

The old priest was wandering too far afield for my understanding, too far from the János system of play. But I said nothing, knowing that he would have to come to his point by his own circuitous route.

'Doubtless, you are asking what all this has to do with roulette.'

'Yes, strange as it may seem to you, Father, some such thought *was* in my mind. But pray continue, for I have still a small reserve of patience to call upon.'

'Has it ever occurred to you to wonder how animals are able unerringly to distinguish friend from foe, real anger from mock anger? Then there is fear, which animals recognize long before we do. Certain it is that they have a sense which we have either never had or have lost somewhere down the endless corridors of evolution. How would you describe that sense?'

'For want of a better word,' I replied, 'I would call it a highly developed sense of smell. Whatever it may be, we have lost it, perhaps because of such a simple thing as being able to recognize facial expressions. Do you agree?'

'Yes, I am inclined to agree, and even if it is not exactly what we call a sense of smell, it is near enough, and whatever it may be, many priests have it, enabling them to tell the true from the false. I can express it no better way.

'That woman, the passing stranger in the confined space of the confessional, gave off an odour which shocked me. It told me that she was false and insincere.'

'Was it an odour you knew, linked to some every-day thing?' I asked.

'No, not precisely. The nearest I have ever approached to it is the disgusting odour of the water in which chrysanthemums have stood for some time. It is associated in my mind with a cemetery after All Saints' Day. My nostrils have twitched with it many times since and they have never misled me.

'People about to utter a lie give off an odour which I can almost always recognize so clearly that I have been able to choke the lie down their throats unuttered. In the confessional, as you may guess, human emotions run the gamut from the peaks of exaltation to the unplumbed depths of despair and, you may believe me, a trained nose can often, not always, identify them. Will you accept this?'

'Willingly, Father. Why not, when your African confrères,

the Zulu witch doctors, are known to be adepts at smelling out their enemies and those who might prove inconvenient.'

I expected an explosion, but it did not come. Although the analogy must have infuriated him, his unshakable honesty would not permit him to deny that it was apt.

'Now let us consider gamblers,' he said. 'Is it possible, will you agree, that this Hungarian is able to classify them by odour? Is it conceivable, do you think, that what has been called chance down all the ages is not the blind, purposeless thing we have tended to assume? Is it possible that what we call the goddess of chance smiles on those who approach her suitably, frowning on those who do not? Then, carrying it one step further, do the successful and unsuccessful suitors for her favours give off distinguishable odours? And, lastly, making due allowance for the inadequacy of the words I have used, has this Hungarian found a moth hole in the curtain which divides us from such mysteries, enabling him to catch a glimpse of what lies on the other side? I do not offer any of these possibilities as well founded and, equally, I refuse to dismiss them as absurdities. You will understand, of course, that my reference to chance as a goddess was purely figurative. As I said, I make no assertions but I wonder.... Yes, I wonder. How do you regard the matter?'

'Having a somewhat pragmatic mind, Father,' I replied, 'it tends to look at the matter with the eyes of scepticism. Let us agree that among gamblers there may well be distinguishing odours as between winners and losers. I see no absurdity in that. The vulgar triumph of a winner may well have an odour easy to detect from the morbid gloom of the loser. But the winner has already won, the loser already lost. The János system, as I call it, separates the losers from the winners in *advance of the fact,* an altogether different matter. How, will you tell me, is it even faintly possible that men and women who, in advance of play, cannot know what the outcome will be, can give off the odour of a prospective winner or loser?'

'And yet, as I understand the matter,' said the old priest, 'the casinos take him seriously enough to put up the bars against him. For this to have happened, there must have been a pattern of success. Also, you must agree, the only known skill of this János is his apparently delicate and unerring sense of smell. Having been a *nez*, it would be strange indeed if this were not the basis of his discovery. I have known a *nez*. He came to Ste Monique when he retired. His eyes saw none of the beauty of Nature. He was tone deaf. He ate only insipid, unseasoned food. Human body odours so disgusted him that he invited nobody into his house. He lived only through this keen, wonderful sense of smell, which never deserted him. In his own field, my friend, never underestimate a *nez*. I know whereof I speak. To a *nez* the impossible is commonplace. The same is true of many people who have one sense developed at the expense of the others. It may well be that this imbalance of the senses produces an imbalance of personality.' The old priest uttered a deep sigh. 'I fear,' he went on, 'we are getting into deep water. Not so long ago anyone who claimed to have penetrated the mysteries of chance would have been burned at the stake. Now, in this age when computers are reaching out into the infinite, who dares to pin the label "impossible" upon anything. What do you intend to do in this matter?'

'I regard this whole matter as I would a new kind of motor-car. I am more concerned to know "Does it work?" than I am to know how it works. Every day I use things which, from experience, I know to be workable. Electricity, for example. But I have not the smallest idea how it works. I have no need to know. So with the János system. If it works, I shall win money. If it does not work, I shall lose some. In either case, knowing how it works will not help me.'

'I find in your attitude an amazing lack of normal curiosity,' observed Father Delorme with pursed lips. 'I do not understand how you can fail to want to know how.'

'You frequently speak of what you call the Grace of God in human affairs. You accept it as a fact. Will you kindly explain it to me in intelligible, everyday terms.'

An explosion of temper ended the discussion, suggesting to me that he also was lacking in normal curiosity, as he called it. We do not lend money on a mortgage without evidence that the house exists and that the mortgagor is the owner. Why should it be held to be impious to require evidence in such a vastly more important matter?

The truth is that the priests have lost their touch, are lagging behind the best lay brains. If they were anything like as confident as they sound when trumpeting from the pulpit, they would welcome honest enquiry by unprejudiced laymen.

The Einstein equation, by means of which man had already begun to probe the infinite, required no priestly inspiration. In the eyes of the priests Darwin and Huxley were not scientists in quest of Truth, but impious charlatans who were rocking the boat.

All this may be a long way from the János system, but if the deity is, as the priests tell us, omnipotent and omniscient, how can certain areas of human activity, such as gambling, be out of bounds? To carry the argument a little further, would it not be a simple matter to arrange for the virtuous to win football pools by way of reward?

'But,' I hear a priestly voice say, 'money is filthy lucre and its possession does not confer happiness.'

Then surely, this being the case, now is the time to abolish offertory boxes and collection plates? We cannot permit filthy lucre to stain the purity of organized religion.

At various times over the years I have advanced such views to Father Delorme. But not any more. His flashpoint is too low and his blood pressure too high and I fear for him. He is in himself a paradox. He is scrupulously honest and highly intelligent yet he preaches absurdities which his intelligence must tell him are sheer poppycock. There is only one explanation: he believes that poppycock can be justified if by swallowing it people are enabled to lead better lives.

He could be right.

6

Where the János system was concerned I was developing
an unfortunate tendency to blow hot and cold. Together
with Esmé and János I made several visits to casinos along
the Riviera, from Cannes to Menton. By following or
opposing players picked out by János, I did win some
money, but not enough to convince me that I might not
just as easily have won it unaided. Nevertheless, I *was*
inclined to believe that he was on the right track, despite the
practical difficulties of operating the system. I was also
inclined to believe with Father Delorme that the basis of the
system was János's highly over-developed sense of smell. I
find nothing incredible in the proposition that under the
influence of certain emotions people give off identifiable
odours, and it seemed reasonable to suppose that to link
these odours to a list of emotions with any sort of accuracy
would require more time and patience than János had been
able to bring to it. But the real stumbling-block to my
acceptance of it all was that winners and losers gave off
these odours in advance of winning or losing. This was
fortune-telling pure and simple. If knowledge of the future
could be gained by the nose, there was no limit to the
possibilities. Mothers of marriageable daughters might employ
János, or people like him, to sniff prospective bridegrooms
for eligibility and compatibility. Personnel managers might
well pick prospective employees by the same method. Doubtless guilt had its own distinctive odour. To use this would be
no more far-fetched than using the lie detector. The witch
doctor method certainly obviated costly trials by jury.

Am I venturing into the realms of absurdity? Perhaps.
But it is impossible to accept the thin end of a wedge such
as János had introduced without facing the possible
consequences of the thick end coming into play.

51

Curiously enough, an apparent failure on the part of János did more to convince me than any of his successes. One evening there came into the Baccara Bar an internationally-known, multi-millionaire speculator. Let the poor chap keep the little which remains of his privacy. While he was drinking an apéritif, János hovered behind him. I am almost sure he was sniffing like a hound on a dead scent. When the man went into the casino, I followed, curious to know how he would play. When Esmé did not follow, I assumed that János had not thought him worth following.

The man took a seat which had been reserved for him at one of the big shemmy tables. Seated there already were three players whom I knew to be big gamblers. For some ninety minutes the play was so big that word went around the casino and a small crowd of spectators gathered. My man won more than I had ever seen won at one session and when he began to lose, much to the annoyance of the other players, he quit. I don't know the extent of his winnings, but my guess would be something over 200,000 new francs, or £14,000.

'I wish I understood why,' János said much later, 'I failed to pick him as a winner.'

'Did he not smell like a winner?' I asked, looking at him narrowly to see the effect of my question, for János had not admitted that his nose was the key to the system.

He maintained a blank poker face, his only acknowledgment being an expressive Gallic shrug.

'Perhaps, if I tell you the man's name, János,' I went on, 'you will understand why you failed. He is so rich that the relatively petty amount he might have lost or won in there tonight could not have touched him emotionally. He just didn't care. There is no smell to a man who doesn't care, is there János?'

'I might have known you would guess,' he said indifferently. 'But even if you tell people, nobody will believe you.'

'Unless you were known to be a *nez*, my dear chap, nobody would have guessed. But it doesn't matter if everyone knows. How many people have your nose? If you were to advertise the fact that your system is to smell winners and losers and that because of this you have been barred by the casinos, they'd be held up to such ridicule that they would want to hide their heads in a hole. Furthermore, you have nothing to fear. What you are doing is strictly legal.'

'That is true,' said János more hopefully, 'but my big trouble now is that my system is not yet perfect. I must make it perfect before I go again to a casino. It seems impossible that I could have failed to pick that rich man as a winner, unless you are right and he just did not care enough.'

It occurred to me some days later that I could provide János with a good proving-ground for his theories, one that could put his mind at rest as well as my own. Five or six times a year I play poker with a few addicts scattered along the Riviera. Two of the school are retired American oilmen, one a French metallurgist, one an Indo-Chinese, a Dane retired from the consular service and myself. It was my turn to be host to the game some days thence. Occasionally we play with seven at the table, but six is a better game.

János jumped at the opportunity to put his theories to the test. The arrangement we made was that he and Esmé should mingle with the players while they had drinks before the game, but would be excluded from the room when play began. Spectators are a nuisance at a poker game. János would set down on paper his predictions as to winners and losers. This in a sealed envelope would be given to me to open when the game broke up. I did not want to take an unfair advantage by perhaps knowing in advance who was going to win or lose, because it would be too easy to play against the unlucky ones and avoid tangling with the lucky ones . . . unless, of course, his nose misled him.

A poker game is only of interest to poker players, so I will spare others the details. As we took our places at the table, Alphonsine came into the room with a tray of drinks, and as she left handed me an envelope which I put in my pocket.

We played until an hour after midnight and when we broke up there was only one big winner, the French metallurgist, a man named Chevrier. The big loser was the Indo-Chinese, whose name I forget. Nobody else could be said to have won or lost any sum worth recording. I lost a trifle.

When the cars drove away János and Esmé joined me and I opened the envelope. On a half sheet of paper János had written: 'Nobody will win or lose much.'

'I'm afraid you are wrong, János,' I had to tell him. 'The Frenchman won nearly a thousand francs, which by the standards of our school is a big win. He won most of this from the Indo-Chinese.'

If I had ever doubted his honesty in this, János now dispelled my doubts, for he sat there in deep dejection, frowning his perplexity. 'I do not understand,' he kept saying. 'I do not understand. Tell me,' he said more brightly, 'would you say that poker is a game of chance?'

'Chance enters into the game,' I replied, 'because the deal is pure chance, but from that point on skill is the deciding factor. The good poker player will almost always beat the poor and indifferent players. But the worst player can hold unbeatable cards. To answer your query, I would say that poker is more than sixty per cent skill and less than forty per cent chance, or luck.'

'Then perhaps that is the answer to my failure this evening,' said János. 'I do not believe that my nose can detect skill.'

In the talk which followed, we tossed around various other ways of putting that famous nose to the test, but there were always practical difficulties. A man who went around a race-course sniffing at horses, jockeys, trainers and owners would soon be ejected.

'What is the real difficulty about casino gamblers?' I asked. 'Most certainly the element of skill is too small to matter.'

'There are too many conflicting odours,' he replied. 'All the odours are subordinated to tobacco smoke, women's perfumes and men's shaving lotions, and individual body odours which have nothing to do with luck. The odours I look for are very subtle and they cannot fight their way through the fog of other odours. . . .'

54

'Then there doesn't seem to be much hope of success,' I said.

'Do not believe that,' János retorted. 'My nose will learn. I must be patient.'

'Wouldn't it be better,' János,' I said, 'to get on with the main business of life and treat this smelling out winners as a hobby?'

'But this is now the main business of my life, don't you see? I cannot return to Grasse. No perfumery would employ me now. What else can I do?'

'Try marrying a rich woman,' I suggested.

'I would do that willingly, but'—he cast an ardent look at Esmé—'my greatest wish is to marry a poor woman.'

'But surely there are one or two little formalities to be attended to before that? Divorce and so forth.'

Esmé at least had the grace to blush. While a young woman can still blush, there is always hope for her.

To avoid being trapped into becoming a marriage counsellor, I brought the talk back to the János system. 'Tell me,' I said, 'are you able to describe these odours given off by the winners and losers?'

'The winners, yes, it is not so difficult. It is like the smell of an excited horse, a young horse that has been some days without exercise. It is being saddled and knows that soon it will have a fine gallop across open country. It is the smell of sweat, but it is nothing like the smell of sweat that comes from a tired horse. . . .'

'And the smell of those who are going to lose?'

'Ah! That is more difficult because it cannot be compared with any well-known smell. It is unpleasant and reminds me of something I have forgotten, but something I should have remembered.'

'Is there, do you know,' I persisted, 'any identifiable smell to people who are desperately anxious to win . . . who must win?'

'Anxiety gives off a special odour,' János replied, 'but whether there is a special odour for gamblers who are too anxious to win, that I do not know.'

55

'Are there special smells of success and failure ... nothing to do with gambling?'

'Yes, I think so ... success especially.'

'Then supposing a man is a professional gambler and is successful, would he smell of success or as a gambler about to win?'

'I believe that there would be a difference, because I believe that every human emotion, mood and characteristic has its own special odour, even though perhaps no nose has yet been sharp enough to detect more than a few. I am not the only one who has thought about such things,' János added. 'Men who have lived more through their sense of smell than through the other senses have been asking these questions for a very long time.

'I have known since I was a child that my sense of smell was abnormally acute, and it was because of that I believed there might be a place for me in the Grasse perfumeries. It was in the library at the Morel perfumery that I read an old parchment document, or a translation of it made by one of the girls who worked there. The document was in Provençal, which I do not understand. It was about an old man named Lamy who lived at Mouans, between Grasse and Cannes, in the sixteenth century. He was put to death for witchcraft because he could read thoughts by way of his nose. He made a powerful enemy by denouncing a man who was planning treachery. When asked how he knew, he said that he could smell it. On other occasions he demonstrated that he could read thoughts so accurately that people were afraid of him. He once warned a friend not to take part in some gambling game because he would be sure to lose. The friend did lose and was ruined. His relations then twisted the warning in such a way that Lamy was accused of causing his friend to lose.

'Learning from Monsieur Morel that my nose excelled that of any other *nez* in Grasse, I set myself to learn whether, outside the perfume business, it could serve me. And it will serve me. Do not doubt it. It may require much more time, but I am not a fool and I will learn.'

János then went on to say that there were forty-two people working in the Morel perfumery and that he learned to know them all by smell, despite the fact that the whole place and everything in it reeked of jasmine.

'The most disturbing smell of all is sexual excitement,' János said, 'because it is everywhere and in the least expected places. Sex is what I call the central smell. It belongs, as you might say, at the middle of the piano keyboard and all the other smells stem from it, up and down the keyboard, if you understand me. Each emotion has its note, or chord, but all are dominated by sex. I was once sitting at a café table in Grasse with a man who was talking angrily about some business associate who, he believed, had robbed him. The odour of anger was strong on him. Then there came along the pavement a very beautiful young woman, a tourist, walking proudly and looking neither to the left nor right. At once the odour of anger went . . . no, not exactly went. It was smothered like a big cloud sweeping over a small cloud and hiding it, by the strong smell of sexual excitement. As the young woman walked away and out of sight, so the big cloud receded until, just as strong as before, my companion gave off the odour of anger.'

'You call anger an odour, but sex a smell. What is the difference?' I asked him.

'To me a smell is altogether animal, like that of a stallion near to a mare in heat. It would not be so unpleasant if it were not so strong . . . occasionally disgusting.'

'It would seem that there are disadvantages, as well as advantages, in being a *nez*,' I said lightly.

'You have never said anything more true,' said János with an expression of disgust on his face. 'Sometimes, even to walk into a hotel bedroom makes me feel sick. At a big cocktail party, or any place where many men and women are together, the sexual excitement is everywhere, killing all the more pleasant odours.'

'What is your favourite odour?' I asked him.

'The odour of nothing such as there is when a clean wind blows across a mountaintop. Then and only then my nose rests for a while. I can then see the beauty of a distant view, hear the sound of sheep bells coming up from the valleys. I am then a more normal person.'

As he spoke János wore a shockingly sad expression on his face, making me realize for the first time that he was a most unhappy man. Like every other Hungarian I ever met, he lived in a minor key. They are saved from utter melancholy by being able to extract happiness from sadness in some twisted way.

The effect of these and other conversations was to convince me that János, even if his ideas regarding gambling were nonsensical, had convinced himself that they were workable. In short, that he was acting in good faith, even if poor sense.

*　　*　　*　　*

It was not hard to see that the attraction which had flared between Esmé and János would soon be, if not already, out of control. Unjustifiably, I felt a certain sense of responsibility, if only because they had met under my roof, and because of an altogether unspecific nod of agreement when asked by Broom, Esmé's father, to keep an eye on her for her own good. Even such a lightly given promise had more weight from the sad fact that the man to whom I had given it was dead. I had been an ass even to nod assent. Broom, with the advantage of a father's authority and the added advantage of holding the purse strings, had not been able to control her. How much less would I, having no standing whatever, be able to succeed where he had failed. Even if I had had full authority, I did not know how to advise her for her own good. The giver and the receiver of advice never view it in quite the same way.

Even if my promise to her father had been of the most binding kind, Esmé would not have accepted it as binding on her.

While I was still turning over in my mind what to do about Esmé and János, if anything, the peace of a lovely afternoon was disturbed by the arrival in my drive of a small semi-racing car with British number plates. It entered at a furious speed and, braking violently at the front door, cut deeply into the gravel. An angry voice which I did not recognize shouted 'Anyone here?'. Alphonsine, who was either out or asleep, did not answer the persistent ringing of the front door bell. After letting the impatient visitor cool his heels for several minutes, I went to see who he was. With goggles lifted from his eyes to his forehead, he was unrecognizable.

'You'd better come back later,' I snarled, 'and don't make such a bloody row and unless you are prepared to arrive at a reasonable speed, stay out altogether.'

As I slammed the door in his face, he was spluttering with rage. He would need to cool down considerably before I listened to him.

'Is Esmé here?' he bellowed.

I was not prepared to give him the lie direct. Equally, believing him capable of violence in the mood he was in, I was not prepared to tell him the truth. 'Even if she were,' I hedged, 'you would have to show a little more courtesy before you got an answer from me. I suggest that when you are in a more reasonable mood you come back ... say around six o'clock.'

It was, of course, Esmé's husband, Latta, Donald Latta I remembered, a man whom in normal circumstances I liked. Controlling his anger with difficulty, he climbed back into the little car. Then, evidently, he changed his mind for I saw from a window his rear view as he strode down the olive walk towards the guest bungalow which he and Esmé had shared during a part of their honeymoon. It was, I decided, just as well. There was nothing I could do to help either of them and there was always the possibility that under the influence of honeymoon memories they might effect a reconciliation. That would be the ideal outcome.

The next thing I knew was the breathless arrival of Alphonsine. 'Does monsieur know that mademoiselle's husband'—Esmé was always mademoiselle to her—'and the Hungarian gentleman are killing each other?'

When I arrived on the scene, János was having the worst

of the encounter. Donald Latta evidently knew how to use his fists, while János had never learned the art and was being badly punished. I may be doing Esmé an injustice, but I had the strong impression that she was enjoying the spectacle. I toyed with the idea of interposing myself between the combatants, but decided against it as being too dangerous. It was not my quarrel and I saw no sense in risking being hurt, although I felt I had to do something.

The issue was soon decided for me when János, blood streaming from cut lips and one eye closed, seemed to crouch into a froglike attitude. As I looked and wondered what he was up to, he appeared to launch himself head first like a projectile, his round bullet head striking Latta on the point of the jaw. There was a horrible click as the Scot was flung on his back to lie motionless. He was out and unconscious, but when I felt his heart, which was beating strongly, I did not worry too much. Between us we carried him to the bed where—as I was to learn a little later—he had caught the guilty couple 'on the job,' as Esmé so delicately phrased it. 'Poor Donald didn't like it . . . much,' she said. 'All the same, he had no business barging in the way he did. What got under his skin was that it was the same bed that he and I had romped in not so long ago. As if it made any difference. But poor Donald, you see, is a sentimentalist and thinks such things are important.'

When 'poor Donald' recovered consciousness and found himself in the bed which was still warm from its previous use, he was understandably annoyed. Quite incoherent in his rage and suffering great pain in the jaw, he struggled to his feet. I led him to the house and put him to bed in the spare room while Alphonsine telephoned for the doctor.

At my insistence Esmé sent János away. I don't much care for my house being used as a brothel, but I'm damned if I'll have it turned into a battlefield.

Reporting to me, the doctor said that Donald's jaw was dislocated and he had lost three teeth. 'He is not fit to be moved for a day or so. Would you like me to send up the village nurse?'

'No, thank you,' I replied, 'his wife is here and quite capable.'

I must set on record to Esmé's credit that for four days and nights, with sleep snatched when she could get it, she nursed Latta with a devotion which had to be seen.

The closing speech of the marriage—for such it was—was in its way a fine performance. 'The doctor is coming to take off the bandages and things, Donald,' she said gently on the morning of the fifth day. 'You'll probably be able to talk then and I'm not waiting for that. You see, my dear, you'll only work yourself into a state and begin lecturing me and ... well, I just can't take any more lectures. They bring out the worst in me and I should probably say more than I mean and regret it afterwards. This way is best. I'm clearing out now and except for an accident, I don't expect we'll meet again. If you want evidence for a divorce, nod your head and I'll see that you have it. Don't waste time trying to find me because it's over, finished and behind us. I expect it's more my fault than yours, but who cares? It was all going to be so wonderful, my dear, but it didn't turn out that way ... and I'm sorry, deeply sorry. Happy landings, Donald, happy landings,' she sobbed piteously as, her face streaming with tears, she made her exit.

61

C

7

'I don't feel up to saying the things I want to say,' Esmé
said as I drove her to Nice airport, 'but I'll write to you one
day soon.'

'Where are you going?'

'To London now. After that I don't know ... or care
much. But I'll turn up again one day like the bad penny ...
that is, if you'll have me.'

'Yes, I expect I'm damned fool enough to have you,' I
said.

Then she was waving goodbye.

When, a day or so after her departure I phoned the house
where János had been staying, only to learn that he had left
for parts unknown, I assumed that he and Esmé had left
together.

As between him and Donald Latta, I tried to maintain a
strict neutrality. Latta was staying with me, but that did not
mean that I was on his side. The fact that he had been
injured gave him his only claim on my hospitality. Had
János been butted into insensibility, I would have felt
obliged to do the same for him. In point of actual fact, my
private sympathies—and I kept them private—were not
with Latta. A man who lets his woman get away from him
reveals himself as an incompetent, while having let her get
away from him, especially a violent-tempered one like Esmé,
he should have had the sense to realize his good fortune. As
a wife, Esmé was no bargain, unless perhaps for a man
prepared to meet violence with violence. Although, as I have
said more than once, I happen to like Esmé more than
ordinarily, I would never have put up with her tantrums
and inability to see any other viewpoint than her own, but
for that ill-understood sense of duty towards her father, from
whom she had inherited her irresponsibility.

The next step in my thinking was to wonder how long János would be able to put up with her, especially as, being a Hungarian, he had an oriental attitude towards her sex. When his patience gave out, as it inevitably would, she would find herself on the receiving end of a walloping she would not forget. Some women liked their men to 'say it with bruises' but I doubted whether Esmé was one of these, so János would be well advised to hide the cutlery first.

Donald Latta, as the injured party, may have been entitled to more sympathy than I was prepared to give him. Liking him had nothing to do with it. He must have been a poor judge of character to suppose that a woman of Esmé's temperament would endure lectures, however well intentioned. There is a thin hair line, not always discernible, dividing lectures from nagging which often outranks more spectacular crimes in the list of unforgivable sins.

Donald Latta's departure for Brazil, where he was engaged on a big construction job, had to be delayed because of his injured jaw. He still entertained vague hopes that Esmé would return to him. I was sure she would not and said so. It seemed kinder to dispel any such idea so that he could go on his way with a sense of freedom from any kind of obligation.

Giving me the Brazilian address, he begged me to let him know if I had news of her. I replied ambiguously, having no intention of doing so. These two had done enough harm to each other without my help to do more. It was with a sense of relief that I watched him go on his way. He would build a good bridge, or dam, whatever it was, but the art of building a happy life seemed to have escaped him. Nothing he did was done smoothly and his departure was in keeping. There is a sharp bend in my drive which needs to be taken at walking speed. Latta, revving up the engine of his wretched little car and making a shattering noise, took it at a furious speed which I won't even guess. There had been rain in the night so a rear tyre tore up the gravel. A pebble, launched as though from a catapult, went through the open dining-room window, smashing a Venetian glass vase in the centre of the table.

Alphonsine, who was in the room when it happened, gave one of the most expressive Gallic shrugs I have ever seen. 'One might have expected something like that,' she said.

And yet, do not let me leave a contrary impression, Donald Latta is an extremely nice chap, although I feel that when his bridge is completed, it will be found that the people on either side of the river would have been better apart.

I think the doctor must have chattered about the events leading to Latta's damaged jaw, for a much garbled version went round the village and foreign community. The arch-garbler, of course, was my *bête noire,* Lady Baskerville, who was quoted to me as having said that Esmé's husband arrived unexpectedly to find me in bed with her. In the altercation which followed, János, the innocent bystander was injured. Fortunately, that viperish old woman's slanders tend to be boomerangs. Nobody, at least nobody who has not an interest in believing ill of me, takes any notice now. But she paid for it. I saw to that.

Observing Lady Baskerville dropping a large pile of laundry at the house of the woman who washes for me, I exclaimed in horror: 'If I had known that you washed that old woman's clothes, I would have sent mine elsewhere.'

'Why?'

'Because I don't want to catch any of those horrible Indian skin diseases, that is why. Be careful you don't catch them.'

Lady Baskerville now sends her laundry to be done in Toulon. Nobody in Ste Monique will touch it with a pole. I have made it my business to make sure she knows why. Now when we meet socially, she gives me one of her con-descending smiles which looks as Eleanor Roosevelt might have looked with a mouthful of unripe gooseberries and mustard. She is not one of my great admirers and she is beginning to realize that in the gentle art of character assassination she is outclassed.

*　　　*　　　*　　　*

During the months which followed it seemed that Esmé had dropped out of my life, for I heard nothing from her. I imagined her touring the world with János, looting casinos as they went. Then one evening, finding the bar prices of the Riviera Casino too steep, I found myself drinking a solitary brandy and Perrier at the Baccara Bar before going in to play. As I was settling down to the evening paper I heard János's voice behind me.

He was talking in a language I could not recognize to a truly lovely young woman, probably a compatriot. Although I could not understand a word, his voice was laden with persuasion, of what kind I could only guess. Whatever it was, she refused to be swayed and went on her way, leaving János in frustrated anger.

'You can't expect them all to fall for you,' I said, joining him.

'This was business,' he said. 'I wanted her to play for me and make some money for herself. But she is too frightened. She will not believe that there is nothing to fear, but the poor girl was brought up in the new Hungary, where secret police hide behind every tree.

'It is a great pity because that one over there'—he indicated a heavy-jowled man of indeterminate nationality—'is going to lose heavily.'

'I've watched him play more than once,' I told János, 'and he often wins.'

'Tonight, my friend, he will lose. . . .'

'Why don't you get Esmé to play for you?'

'I have not seen Esmé since the day when her husband surprised us. It was most embarrassing. I suppose,' he added, going off at a tangent, 'that you wouldn't care to play for me?'

'Why not?'

'All right. You play with your money and we go fifty-fifty on what you win.'

'Go to hell! You add your 500 francs to mine and we go fifty-fifty. *Entendu?*'

He didn't like it, so I supposed that he had been finding cut-rate stooges to play for him.

I found my man at the *trente et quarante* table, where by the nature of the game it would be easy to play against him without being conspicuous.

Most of the time he played with 500-franc plaques, occasionally doubling, but at the end of half an hour he was about even. So was I. When he bet 500 francs, I bet 100 and when he doubled, so did I. On three consecutive hands he won, causing me to harbour doubts about the János system. Then he lost on eight consecutive hands, which meant that I won. For more than an hour he was like a man climbing a ladder, up two rungs and down three. With a good reserve behind me, I doubled my stakes and went on winning.

My man got up from the table in disgust and crossed to the 'big' roulette table, where he began scattering money about the board like a drunken sailor. Most of the time it was impossible to play against him. Once, when he had covered eleven single numbers as well as various combinations, it seemed that only zero was left uncovered. I put 100 francs on it, standing to win 3,500. The ball dropped into the slot of zero. My man then called it a day, having dropped the proverbial packet. At the settlement with János, which we arranged well away from the casino precincts, we divided 13,000 francs , or about £910.

'Well, what do you think of the János system now?' he asked triumphantly.

'It looks easy,' I replied.

'It *is* easy. Let us be partners and we will die rich.'

I wasted a full hour trying to convince him that my refusal was not a reflection on him personally, but for a dozen other reasons.

'But you want money ... everyone wants money,' he said indignantly.

'I want money,' I told him, 'but I am not prepared to pay too much for it.'

'As you have seen,' he said with a bewildered expression

on his face, 'it is not possible for me to cheat you. It is only possible for you to cheat me ... and I do not believe you would do that.'

I know that as I tried to make him see my viewpoint I must have typified the smug Englishman as so many Europeans see him. I face the possibility that my own countrymen reading these lines may share this view. But it can't be helped, and so long as it does not stop them from buying my next book, who cares?

'You see, János,' I said, 'I am in some ways a very lucky man. I am able to do what so few people are able to do: I live as I want to live. I can call myself rich because I have enough money to provide me with my simple wants. Nobody is dependent on me. I have no debts. Also, my need for money grows less every year. My days of chasing lovely young women are over. That is the greatest economy any normal man ever effects in his life.

'Now you come along to dazzle me with the prospect of more money ... at a price. Instead of roulette being a game which I enjoy, it would become hard work. On evenings when I would prefer to sit at home and read a book, which means most evenings, I would find myself in a casino because of my bloody partner. I know every casino on the coast and I don't have to walk in backwards to pretend I am going out. I may have blotted my copybook many times but never in a casino or over gambling. If your system is what you believe it to be, I expect we would win a few thousands before they tumbled to us, but you may believe me, János, I find the price too high.'

Then he said something straight from the heart: 'Yes I think I understand, but what you do not understand is that it is still easy to be an Englishman, not so easy to be a young Hungarian with no friends or influence on this side of the Iron Curtain. We Hungarians are like the Jews. To succeed at anything we have to be twice as clever as anybody else. It is not always easy.'

It was time we spoke of other things.

'All these months,' I told him, 'I have taken it for granted that you and Esmé went off together. Now you tell me you have not seen her. Have you heard from her?'

Neither of us had. I had the impression that János was bearing her absence with great fortitude, but I could have been wrong for, like most Hungarians I have met, he wore a mask which revealed little.

The next time I saw him he was deep in conversation at the Baccara Bar with a well-known Englishwoman whose face was—and is—familiar to the readers of the shiny society weeklies, almost always with horses in the background. She had a long equine face and slightly protruding teeth. Her brother is an impoverished peer, although impoverished is the wrong word, implying as it does that he once had money and no longer has any. The family has lived on the fringe since an eighteenth century forbear gambled away his patrimony. About the only solid fact I know about the brother is that his tailor, who happens to be my tailor, will not release a suit to him until it has been paid for.

János, from snatches of their talk wafted my way, was instructing the lady in her duties. Not wishing to interrupt, I went into the casino, where for about an hour I played my usual small game of roulette with indifferent success. At the 'big' table I found myself facing the lady, but I could not follow her play because I did not know whom János had sniffed out for her to follow or oppose. But it was apparent that she was winning steadily in fairly large sums. Then, increasing her stakes, as a good gambler should when playing with the casino's money, she brought off the coup known as *zero et chevaux*, 100 francs on zero and 100 each on 01, 02 and 03. Zero won and nearly 9,000 francs were pushed across to her, to disappear into a capacious handbag. She let the stakes lie where they were and on the next spin of the wheel 3 was the winner at odds of 17 to 1, a net win of 1,400 francs, or roughly £100.

Although the lady would never see fifty again, she managed to shed some twenty years as her eyes danced and her lips quivered with excitement and pleasure. Looking at her then in her little moment of triumph, one had a backward glance at what she might well have been before life had soured her.

Some of those at the table, hard-boiled casino habitués, smiled their pleasure at her win. Their keen perceptions saw through the façade of three-year-old finery and a diamond brooch the colour of an amber traffic light which might have been taken for a topaz. Such people as she seldom won. Her need to win was against her. Yet she had won and went on winning. *La boule passe* came the cry as the croupier slipped out of his seat to make way for a colleague. Most gamblers enjoying a winning streak quit when this happens, believing that it ends the run. Either my *vis-à-vis* had never heard of the superstition, or disregarded it, for to the amazement of the players around her she went on winning.

When she finally stopped playing, the chips were spilling out of her bag and the man who empties the ashtrays had to help her carry the rest of her winnings to the change desk to be turned into notes. As I left the casino a huge pile of chips was in process of being counted.

'You'll be pleased to hear that your girl-friend has won a packet for you,' I told János when I went into the Baccara Bar again. 'Is it a 50–50 deal?'

'No, because I provided all the capital. It's 60–40 . . . in my favour, of course.'

'That seems fair enough. I'll join you after she's reported and you've divided the loot. It looks as though the János system is coming into its own.'

I went to a table on my own and resumed reading the evening paper over my drink. For the first time since he assumed power I found myself in full agreement with General de Gaulle, who had reiterated his determination to keep the U.K. out of the Common Market, and I hoped that he would succeed. I have still to meet a Frenchman who regards our entry as anything but a disaster. We played the balance of power game too skilfully and for too long to win any European friends except among the smaller nations.

It struck me, looking up from the paper, that János's stooge was taking the hell of a long time to count her winnings. János evidently thought so too, for he began to fidget, glancing uneasily towards the entrance.

When at long last the lady arrived, she smiled brightly at János as she joined him at the table. 'We had quite a nice little win,' she said. 'Shall we divide it here, or somewhere more discreet?'

'How much?' he asked in a gravelly voice.

'Nearly a thousand francs.'

'Each or between us?'

'Between us, of course.'

I have never seen a cobra hypnotize a dove, but what followed must have been of the same order. Fixing her in an icy gaze, János surveyed her insultingly from top to toe, his face as he did so becoming a Mongol mask, eyes narrowing to slits and skin stretched almost to breaking point across his prominent cheekbones. There was menace in every line of him.

'Think again,' he said.

'I don't know what you mean,' she said, the whites of her eyes showing all round the irises in fear. 'Don't look at me like that.'

'Think again!'

Trying to carry it off with a high hand, she started to get up from the table.

'Sit down!' said János softly, looking at her with sheer ferocity. 'You surely don't suppose I am such a fool as to let you play for me without having you watched? I know to within a few hundred francs what you won in there. You are not dealing with an Englishman, you know. I am not a gentleman. I am a Hungarian. You are not a lady. You are a thief.'

'I won't stay here to be insulted.'

'You will stay until you have given me my money and I have told you that you may go.'

Her indecision was plain to see, but she remained seated. János, meanwhile, withdrew from his pocket a small blue phial, which he placed very carefully on the table. The unhappy woman gazed at it in bewildered fascination, hardly able to take her eyes off it.

'Give me my money,' said János.

Summoning all her courage, she stood up. 'If you try to stop me I shall ask the man behind the bar to telephone for the police.'

'Long before the police arrived here I would have knocked out those big ugly teeth. Then, to teach you not to steal, I would break every finger on both your hands. You doubt it? Then call the police and see.'

The wretched woman was terror-stricken, torn between the anguish of parting with her ill-gotten money and fear of what she read in the inscrutable Hungarian face threatening her. János did not look as though he made idle threats. Then, in the overworked word, he was positively sinister.

János's cold anger at the barefaced attempt to cheat him was matched by the woman's frenzied determination, having managed to lay her hands on more money than she had seen for years, not to part with it. It was a case of the irresistible force meeting the immovable object. Which of them would win? My inclination was to believe that she would. She was in possession of the money. To take it from her would be robbery with violence. She was a woman of title, even if a somewhat shopsoiled one, while he was a rootless Hungarian without any influence. Of the two, she was the more likely to be believed.

The only possible witness of the true nature of their bargain was myself, which would put me in an impossible position if it came to a showdown. The thought of having to testify against her appalled me, but there would have been no escape from it.

I am tempted to say that this confrontation lasted five minutes, which I realize is absurd. It just seemed like that. I watched her while she searched the inscrutable face of János for some sign of relenting, but the blazing eyes boring at her grew more, rather than less, ferocious.

Twice I saw her fingers move towards the catch of her handbag. Twice they dropped limply, more eloquent than words. That thick wad of notes would enable her to pay off embarrassing debts, buy clothes to replace the outdated things she wore, enjoy a little luxury and, best of all, give her a little respite from worry. Greed and fear balanced each other on the scales but, even as I watched, fear became the winner. Whatever it was she read in the face confronting her gave her a foretaste of what to expect if she continued to assert her claim to the money. I think she realized, as I began to, that she must be prepared to face violence. Whether János would resort to violence because of the amount involved—and my guess put it at between two and three thousand pounds—or because of the principle of the thing, I did not . . . could not know. But having come to know János much better since then, I would say it was a mixture of the two.

'I am waiting,' he said in an icy voice.

'If I give you your share now, can I keep mine?' she asked, in a voice which quavered.

'Give it all to me. I do not make bargains with thieves.'

As hope drained from her eyes and the blood from her cheeks, she opened the catch of her handbag, withdrawing from it a thick roll of notes wrapped in a scarf, which she handed to János.

'You can go now,' he said.

'I cannot go back to my hotel without the money to pay the bill,' she said piteously.

'Then do not go back. Go to another hotel. Go anywhere, so long as it is out of my sight.' Peeling off a few uncounted notes from the wad, he tossed them contemptuously on the table. 'Now I understand what is meant by *noblesse oblige*. I have often wondered. If,' he went on in her hearing, turning to me, 'she is a good sample of your English aristocracy, no wonder you want to get rid of them. They are as bad as the Hungarian kind.'

'A good half of the fault was yours, János,' I said at length. 'A woman of her class who made such a deal with you was bound to be desperate for money. You put temptation in her way and it was too much for her. Anyway, your idea of

72

having stooges play for you is bound to fail and for the same reason.'

'Yes, I am afraid you are right,' he said. 'Is nobody honest?'

'I would bet anything I possess that Esmé was straight with you, down to the last centime. . . .'

'Ah! Esmé, yes,' he said feelingly. 'With Esmé I would conquer the world.'

'And you wouldn't know what to do with it. You are too greedy for money, or something. If you will only be content with winning reasonable sums, without drawing attention to yourself, you can probably live the rest of your life in luxury. Don't think that this evening's little drama will have gone unobserved. Make up your mind that for some long time you will have made this coast too hot to hold you.'

'I shall have to go somewhere where I can play myself,' he said lugubriously.

'Where?'

'England, perhaps. Is the gambling straight there?'

'I don't know. I have only been in one of the clubs and it appeared to be well conducted. But it was owned by crooks. The smell of American gangsterism is strong over British gambling, but with your nose it shouldn't be hard to detect.'

8

Coincidence has been described as the most cowardly device of the writer of fiction, ranking with thunderstorms as a way of making the heroine swoon into the hero's arms, with the doubtful privilege of regretting it ever after. With this view I feel bound to agree, if only because the coincidences of real life transcend those of fiction for sheer improbability. Thus, I attach no importance, see no hidden hand of Fate, to the fact that a letter from Esmé asking where she could find János came in the same delivery as one from him asking where he could find her. After some deliberation I decided that in having introduced them in the first place, I had done enough. It was my considered opinion that these two were not good for each other, and while I would do nothing active to keep them apart, I would not help bring them together again. If they were really determined to seek each other out they would succeed without my help, and if they were not so determined, that told its own story. I find that many people, even the majority, are predictable except in the most bizarre circumstances. But not so either of these two.

When the two letters had lain on my desk for three days while I was considering how to reply, I dropped them in the wastepaper basket. Esmé had written from an address in Kensington, where she was in attendance on her mother, while János wrote from Monte Carlo where, with some little success, he was exploring the possibilities of craps as a means of exploiting his system. He must have been doing well because he invited me to go there at his expense.

Craps, or African golf, is a purely American game to the best of my knowledge. It is played with two dice, and although I have played on odd occasions, I do not understand its niceties.

Being a game of pure chance, unless 'educated dice' are introduced into it, craps was ideal for János's purpose. One sentence in the letter suggested that the sands were running out fast in Monte Carlo; 'I may not be here much longer as some very dirty looks are cast in my direction.'

'Mother is not well and wants me to stay,' said Esmé, 'but I have had about enough, I can't be as sympathetic as I might have been if she had ever behaved decently to Father. She warns me against seeing any more of you, considering you a bad influence. Anybody my father liked was, according to her, a bad influence. Anyway, bad influence or not, will you lend me some money?'

A wiser man than I counselled against lending, or borrowing, as a sure way of losing friends. Most would-be borrowers, I find, are so reckless with the truth that I find myself losing all sympathy. Except in the case of a great friend, I will not lend money unless there seems a good chance of getting the borrower out of trouble altogether. I will not lend money to pay pressing debts. Let the creditors wait. If the debtor has no money they can't get it out of him.

Lending money to Esmé, if I were ass enough to do so, would be pouring it down a drain. The fact that the appeal came from the hotel where she was staying with her mother was evidence that she had tried a touch and failed. Mother knew best. Or, if she didn't, she ought to.

Esmé and her brother had inherited a vast property in Central America measured in hundreds of square miles, which had been in the family since the time of the Conquistadors. Neither she nor her brother ever wanted to see the place again and although it was immensely rich, potentially so if not in fact, it apparently yielded nothing. It was up to one or both of them to visit the place and turn it into cash to take care of their immediate necessities.

The next I heard of János was that he had arrived in Ste Monique and was staying with his friends. When I met him in the village he renewed his urging for me to join him in Monte Carlo where, he assured me, he would prove to my satisfaction that his system was what he claimed for it.

'Thanks all the same,' I said, 'but I'm still not interested. Even less interested than before. I dislike Monte Carlo and don't want to spend an unnecessary hour there.'

'What is wrong with Monte Carlo?' he asked in amazement.

'A lot of things. It's full of people who hate the place, to whom its only attraction is that there is no income tax, which isn't a good enough reason for living anywhere.'

Evidently this was a new thought to János, for he said with a puzzled air: 'What is your reason for living in Ste Monique? You see, for me and for many Hungarians who have left Hungary, it is enough to live. Where we live is not so important.'

I was tempted to reply in some detail, but refrained. Being able to live wherever it pleased me, with the comforting knowledge that I could always return to my own country if I wished to, made me a privileged person in the eyes of someone like János. He, if he blotted his copybook in France, or anywhere else, would be deported to Hungary. Having left there illegally, the consequences might be anything from unpleasant to fatal. He had to live dangerously in order to live at all, and his best hope for the future was to amass a sum of capital as a bulwark against the buffets of fortune. I was beginning to understand why he clung so fervently to the János system. Having no work permit, no job was open to him.

'Have you seen Esmé?' he asked at length.

Since it was phrased in just that way, I was able to reply truthfully that I had not.

The decision as to whether or not to put these two in touch with each other again was soon taken out of my hands by the arrival one morning of a taxi from Toulon. The driver, evidently a student of human nature, declined to bring the baggage into the house until he had been paid. I need not add that Esmé was his passenger. 'You don't seem very pleased to see me,' she remarked.

'Your perceptions are very acute for such an early hour.'

'So would yours be if you had sat hard-arsed for eighteen

hours on slow trains from Calais. Just now I need a warm bath, a drink and twelve hours' sleep. The lecture can wait, can't it?'

'There won't be any lecture,' I assured her, 'just a warning. Don't bring men in. If your urges become too strong for you, please fornicate elsewhere. Your morals are your own affair and I would not dream of trying to censor them. It's just that I don't like my house being treated like a "hot pillow" motel.'

Looking woebegone and bedraggled after the long and uncomfortable train journey, Esmé followed Alphonsine dejectedly down to the guest bungalow. She had lost some of her bounce. There had been plenty, so she could spare it. Perhaps life was succeeding where people had failed to tame her.

Alphonsine was soon fussing with a tray for Esmé's breakfast. *'La pauvre chère!'* she murmured. 'Nothing to eat since yesterday morning! Sitting up all night without proper sleep!'

'She is young and probably enjoyed the experience,' I said, 'and do not forget that I live here too and that I have not yet had breakfast.'

In so many ways Esmé was impossible . . . selfish, rude, wild, irresponsible and indifferent to the opinions of others. On due reflection I doubt whether her morals, that is to say her sexual morals, were anything like as bad as I may have suggested. Indeed, judging from what I see, hear and read, I am inclined to believe that hers were considerably better than average. She had a sort of hard core of fearless integrity which forbade her to claim virtues which she did not possess. Equally, she was not furtive. One evening when she was nursing her husband, after he had been butted by János, she and I were chatting before turning in. 'It was darned unfortunate that Donald chose just that moment to arrive on the scene . . . unfortunate for him. I don't care a damn. But he's so prim and proper that he just can't understand that a girl needs a little sex from time to time to stop the corners of her mouth from turning down.'

Than which I never heard a more honest and unaffected statement of the case.

The other thing I like about Esmé is that she never crawls. Being under an obligation to me did not stop her from being as rude as she pleased, and when I repaid her in kind, she was more amused than upset.

Inevitably, Esmé and János met again within a few days of her arrival. Ste Monique is too small for it to be otherwise. 'Are you two serious about each other?' I asked her on one occasion.

'Do you mean are we going to get married?' I nodded.

'There's lots of time to think about that. There's the problem of divorce, too. All three of us are Catholics . . . of a kind. Only Donald is a real one. He won't divorce me, but as I understand it, he doesn't mind me divorcing him. If I care to risk my immortal soul by re-marrying, that's all right with him. But he would still consider our marriage as binding on us. A funny way of looking at it, don't you think?'

'All that is going to take time, which is perhaps all to the good. It will anyway stop you doing anything hasty.'

'For more than one good reason, I won't marry János. If I ever re-marry it will be because I want children. If Donald and I had ever had children, they would have been all right, I believe. Anyway, they would have stood a good chance of being normal. His stolid Scotch respectability would have watered down my . . . Mother calls it wildness, or whatever it is I got from Father's side of the family. They were all mad as hatters.

'I've played with the idea of marrying János, but I'll never do it. He's a nice chap. I like him very much and if I set myself to it, I could easily fall in love with him. But what holds me back is the question of children. I'm wild enough and know it, but at heart János is a bandit, and the mixture of the two wouldn't give the kids a fair chance in life. It wouldn't be fair on the world either. There are enough bastards in circulation without adding to them.'

'Don't make your family out to be worse than they were. . . .'

'I couldn't. They were real Grade A prize stinkers. How

78

otherwise did they get hold of a tract of land the size of a big English county? Bought it? They never bought anything they could steal. . . .'

'Coming back to János,' I urged her, 'if you are not going to marry him, when and if you are free, wouldn't it be easier to drop him . . . now?'

'My dear Steve, you don't seem to understand my position. My mother, who has tons of money, says I'll have to get a job. My brother Pedro, who's a throwback and is nearly as respectable as Donald, invites me to come and keep house for him. I told him to stuff it. I could get a job . . . of sorts. As you know, I was an assistant buyer for a short time in London. But I've no talent for it and once was enough. My bottom was black and blue through being pinched by nasty little men who, if I jumped into bed with them, *might* help with my career.

'I imagine you don't want to adopt me, do you? If you do, say so now. That leaves me the choice between János and becoming a whore, and of the two I prefer János. You see, Steve, he's got something. That nose of his may make a few mistakes, but it's right more often than not and, so long as he doesn't walk down any dark alleys at night, we shall be sitting pretty. People don't care for a man who wins too often and I gather there have been some very nasty things said about him in Monte Carlo. They jump to the conclusion . . . the wrong one . . . that he cheats. But the joke is that he doesn't have to.'

'Meaning that he would if necessary?'

'I don't know, or care. I believe that in life we do as we must. Can you disagree with that?'

'So long as you don't assert it quite so sweepingly, you are probably very near the mark. But there is a leaven of people in the world that still lives decently for decency's own sake and . . . well, it's a thought to cling to in a world whose standards are on the toboggan slide. And even if you are right, you are too young to have reached your conclusions. You must have been associating with the wrong kind of people.'

*   *   *   *

79

I am only too well aware that on the subject of what I call the János system I don't seem able to make up my mind. One day I am inclined to believe that his nose is the wonderful instrument it must be if his claims for it are valid, while on the next day my naturally sceptical mind rejects it as poppycock. He has enjoyed a run of luck, which can come to anyone, and to see any more in it than that is sheer self-deception. Let me add that neither view of the matter had anything whatever to do with my refusal to enter into some sort of partnership with János. That was based on nothing more nor less than a great distaste for becoming involved in such a fringe activity. I just don't need to.

But all this is a long way from saying, or giving the impression, that I was not interested. I was and am fascinated by the whole business if only for the reason that if János's claims were well-founded, he had extended the frontiers of human knowledge.

Chance has always been regarded as a mathematical concept, along with the laws of probability, and has been inseparable from a lot of hocus-pocus from the Roman augurs and before, to divination by chicken entrails down to tea leaves. Chance in the latter event becomes Luck, although only by endless hair-splitting can they be differentiated. Now comes a young Hungarian who propounds the preposterous theory that Chance not only casts a kind of shadow before it, but that the nature of the Chance is detectable by its odour. If right in his contention it is a poor look-out for soothsayers, necromancers, crystal gazers and the hunchbacks who lurk outside casinos for the gullible to touch them.

Anyone putting forward such a theory would incur laughter for his pains, but János, even if he had not proved his case, had tangible evidence in the shape of hard cash to suggest that he had been able to overcome unfavourable odds and make a profit.

Could he continue to do so? My curiosity demanded an answer.

At this time I received an air mail letter from Australia which caused me to revise my personal plans. It was from a woman who, in the dim long ago, had been my secretary. When I left the business world she became secretary to a shipping tycoon in London and for years continued to look after my affairs in a variety of small matters, collecting money due to me, buying odds and ends and sending them to France, digging out information of various kinds. Then she married, this was just before the war. She and her husband went to Australia. There a daughter was born in, I think, 1938 or 1939. About twenty years later the daughter, whom I never met, married and produced a son, dying in childbirth. Then my ex-secretary, whose married name was Whitgift, was widowed. She took over the grandson, Peter, and brought him up. She—her first name was Ann—brought the boy back to England with the intention of living there, but finding the climate too much for her, went back to Australia, staying with me at Ste Monique en route before catching her ship at Genoa. Over the years Ann and I had corresponded regularly and had become friends. There are few people living towards whom I feel so warmly disposed. Her letter was to say that she would avail herself of the open invitation always extended to her to bring Peter to stay with me before going on to England to visit various relatives.

I cancelled a trip I had planned, and some two weeks after I received the letter was at Nice airport to meet them. Ann and Peter took over the guest bungalow while Esmé, greatly to her annoyance, moved into my guest-room in the house. The arrangement worked reasonably well until Esmé, discovering that my bathroom was better than hers, began to use it, leaving it in a filthy mess. I scotched that by keeping it locked and was called a selfish bastard for my pains.

Happily, my three guests got on well together. Peter was a tough but likeable little so-and-so, despite a total absence of manners.

One of the first fruits of the visit was our initiation by Peter into the Australian game of 'two-up', said to be the only gambling game ever invented at which cheating is impossible.

Two-up is played with two pennies placed tails up on a

flat piece of wood like a six-inch ruler. On a patch of bare earth a length of string is strung between two uprights at a height of about eight feet. The players bet against a banker. The two pennies are tossed from the flat piece of wood over the string. If two tails turn up, the bank loses. If two heads turn up, the bank wins. A head and a tail, no bet. The pennies are always tossed from the flat strip of wood tails up in order to prove that they are not double-headed. In Australia the introduction of double-headers is unwise to the point of being dangerous. It is a sure way to the casualty department of the nearest hospital.

Ann Whitgift came upon the scene one day while Peter, aged twelve, was initiating Esmé, János and me into the niceties of the game. 'I hope you don't disapprove,' I said, observing her lifted eyebrows.

'It wouldn't do much good if I did,' she replied wryly. 'He's an Australian and they are all gambling crazy. But I do implore you to make him pay if he loses.'

'I would have done that anyway,' I told her.

János was delighted with two-up for here, if there ever were one, was a game of pure chance without any element of skill.

9

Ann Whitgift was most co-operative when it was explained to her that we wanted to use Peter, her grandson, as a guinea-pig in a series of experiments. 'Is this for real, or is it some elaborate legpull?' she asked when I told her of János's remarkable olfactory prowess.

'No, it's no legpull,' I assured her. 'János believes and I am more than half inclined to agree, that he can separate the winners and the losers by using his over-developed sense of smell to detect them. As you can well see, if one knows in advance which of a group of people is going to win and which will lose, there is, ready-made, an infallible gambling system. The question now is, do you mind Peter being used to test these theories?'

'I suppose that depends on just how you are going to set about it,' she said. 'I don't think you can corrupt him by turning him into a gambler because he's already corrupted. He'll gamble on flies walking up a wall. At his school they all gamble. Just what is involved?'

'Well, without letting Peter know that there is an experiment, we want to play two-up . . . play it for money.'

'How much money?'

'How much has he got?' I asked. 'It is an essential part of the experiment that he must stand to win enough to excite his cupidity, if any. . . .'

'He qualifies there all right, the money-grubbing little so-and-so!'

'. . . and enough for it to hurt a bit if he loses. We don't want you to give him any, because that would defeat the whole purpose of the experiment. How much money of his own does he possess now?'

'In the savings bank, or in his pocket?'

'In his pocket.'

'Various relations and friends gave him small sums ... ten bobs and so on, before we left. I'd say he has around five pounds.'

'And you don't mind if we win it off him?'

'I'd be pleased rather than otherwise. It might prove to be a salutary lesson and teach him that money doesn't grow on trees. He can calculate odds quickly, but he doesn't really understand the value of money yet. Hardly surprising when you remember that he's only twelve years old.'

When I told János and Esmé about Ann's helpful attitude, János made one stipulation. 'Peter's a dirty little bastard and I don't think he's had a proper bath since he left home. Please ask Mrs Whitgift to see that he has a proper bath, using unscented soap. He smells as if he'd been swimming in a sewer.'

I put this to Ann somewhat less forcibly and she said it didn't surprise her because he was just old enough to resent any woman, even his grandmother, superintending his ablutions. 'Tell János he'll have to do his own dirty work,' she said. 'I expect you'd better be on hand, too, to hold him. To tell you the truth I *had* noticed that he was a bit gamey.'

The air of his homeland must have imbued Peter with a sturdy independence of thought and action, for despite the most earnest persuasions, Peter did not take at all kindly to the idea of a bath. In a land where long droughts were the rule rather than the exception he cannot have been accused of wasting precious water. 'Why should I bath when I don't want to?'

'Because you are being asked to ... nicely so far,' I replied.

'What's it to you anyway?'

'You are living in my house, Peter, eating at my table. Surely, if only as a mark of respect, you can afford to be clean?'

'Why should I respect you?'

Why indeed?

'Come on! Let's play two-up.'

'No bath, no two-up,' I told him firmly.

'Why?'

84

'Because you stink like a polecat, that's why.'

'What's a polecat?'

'Grow two more legs and then look in a mirror.'

'Yah! Bloody funny!'

'Don't swear at me.'

'Bloody's not swearing. You should hear. . . .'

I gave up. János took over. He took over in masterly fashion. In Hungary, it seems, they know how to deal with recalcitrant youths. Seized firmly by the right ear, the one which was more prominent, he became relatively—note the word relatively—docile. While I know it is the current fashion to ride rough-shod over whatever delicate suscept-ibilities the reader has retained, I flatly decline to set down on paper the things which this twelve-year-old hellion called János. A firm twist of the right ear checked the flow of invective, which was painfully repetitive.

'Be quiet,' said János silkily. 'The sooner you have taken off all your clothes, the sooner I will stop twisting your ear.'

The water running into the bath drowned some of the boy's flowers of speech.

'Now, Peter, listen to me,' said János. 'If you will promise to soap yourself thoroughly all over, I will let go of your ear. . . .'

'Go and up yourself!'

'Very well. If you prefer to do it the hard way, then we will do it the hard way. I shall now hold your head under the water. When you are tired of it and indicate that you will behave yourself by tapping the side of the bath, I will allow you to breathe. . . .'

Still held by the ear and roaring obscenities, Peter found himself flung expertly into the bath and, his head submerged, there followed a merciful silence.

I did not time the total immersion with a stop-watch, but I would say that twenty seconds, which is a long time, passed before there was a tap on the side of the bath.

'Will you wash yourself now, or shall I call in Alphonsine to do it? Please yourself.'

For the first time Peter looked really frightened. Between him and Alphonsine there had been a state of undeclared war since his arrival. Alphonsine regarded him as a savage because he did not speak a word of French and had the table manners of an untrained bull-terrier. He regarded her as a terrifying being because she spoke not a word of English and had a tufted wart on her chin which waggled when she gabbled French. When I offered to fetch Alphonsine, Peter surrendered.

I dare say that a student of child psychology would understand why, from that moment onward, Peter's attitude to me and to János changed. The little politeness I was accorded was so grudging as to be insulting, while he and János became great buddies. Forgotten, apparently, was the fact that János had practically twisted his ear off. If, as I was sometimes sorely tempted to do, I had taken the buckle end of a belt to him, I wondered whether he would have felt more warmly disposed to me.

Peter, I am bound to admit, was one of my failures. János, almost without effort, had tamed him. Alphonsine likewise. On one occasion Peter had the temerity to creep into the kitchen on larceny bound, attracted by the savoury smells of cooking. This was something Alphonsine would not tolerate. The sharp slaps as she boxed his ears violently were audible in the front of the house. But despite the barrier of language between them, they became thereafter quite friendly. I heard Alphonsine refer to Peter as 'Le pauvre petit' one morning, having just made him a cup of chocolate.

But I digress. Soon after Peter had been bathed and deodorized, we assembled for the game of two-up. János, having given him the once-over by nose, told me quietly: 'The boy will lose.'

'Then let's take the little bastard for his shirt,' I said. I was not warmly disposed.

'That would be very foolish,' retorted János, 'for if he has no money we cannot continue the experiments. Today we must keep the stakes small. Let him lose only enough to prove that my nose was not wrong.'

The two-up school comprised Ann Whitgift, Esmé, János, myself and Peter. The currency was francs. Peter surprised his grandmother by producing the equivalent of £13 to be changed, instead of her estimated £5.

Peter lost steadily in sums of one and two francs. He was a good gambler, understanding the folly of chasing his losses. When he had lost a third of his capital he announced that it was not his day and that he would win it all back and more on the morrow. At the insistence of János we agreed not to play again until the boy smelled like a winner. It was three days before this happened. In the meantime we had to submit to being called unsporting, triple-distilled bastards for not allowing him his revenge.

It has been said that English children are too inhibited for their characters to develop. I have not noticed it, certainly not for many years. A powerful magnifying glass would have been needed in order to find Peter's inhibitions.

Time was running out. Soon Peter and his grandmother would be on their way to London. We arranged, therefore, much to the boy's delight, to play twice and sometimes three times daily. The results, while not absolutely conclusive, tended to support the János theories.

On every occasion when Janos's nose told him Peter would be a loser, he was a loser. On five occasions János predicted that the boy would win, but on only three did he do so. To me the most interesting result obtained was when János could detect no winner's or loser's odour. 'All I can smell is dirty small boy,' he said. There had been two days without a bath. On these occasions, without exception, Peter emerged from the game a mere trifle up or down.

The rest of us were tested for smell also. Ann Whitgift was consistently 'neutral' in smell, which I interpreted, I think rightly, as meaning she had no interest in winning or losing, although in fact she was the most consistent winner. Esmé gave off the odour of a loser and only won once. Only once was I pronounced a winner in advance and I did win some seventy francs, which was a lot considering the low stakes of the game. On all the other days my gains and losses were minimal, losses predominating.

'I learned more from Peter than from the rest of you,' János announced after Peter had gone to bed on the day of the last game, 'and it confirms my belief that the amount at stake and how much it means to the individual are the deciding factors. Peter was the biggest gambler amongst us because winning or losing meant more to him, he having less money to lose than any of us.'

Having brought out so plainly the less lovable aspects of the boy, it seems only fair to say that these were the more apparent because he made no smallest effort to hide them. But underneath his not very attractive exterior, he had many good qualities. He had a good sense of humour, the kind that enabled him to see a joke against himself. He gambled like a gentleman. Nobody could tell from his manner and behaviour whether he was winning or losing. That, to my mind, is high praise. I liked, too, his frank and fearless spontaneity of utterance, which may not in the future win him many friends, but will enable him to walk upright. I imagine that when he begins to chase women and he observes them flinching from his gameyness, the penny will drop, and he will realize that soap and water have their uses.

All in all, I predict a bright future for Peter.

In view of his contribution to the development of the János system, even though an unwitting contribution, I felt it only fair to tell him that, provided it could be obtained locally, he could have anything he liked for his last dinner with me. By way of showing his appreciation he bathed voluntarily, which I thought was a gracious response.

'If I were you,' said his grandmother, 'I would qualify the offer by saying that the rest of us won't feel bound to eat his choice unless we like it.'

It was a merciful afterthought, for Peter's choice was canned sardines, which he proceeded to mash up on his plate with the best part of a jar of apricot jam, this followed by strawberry ice cream. The little speech he gave afterwards, thanking me for my hospitality in general and in particular the last meal, was a model of its kind. I wish I could quote it verbatim. Only one false note was struck. This was when, resuming his seat, he sneezed and farted simultaneously.

Esmé and I drove them to Nice airport. Said quickly, it sounds nothing, but the fact remains that the return journey approximates 140 miles. Truth to tell, I am getting a little tired of it. I long ago served warning on intending guests that if they avail themselves of cheap night flights they must make their own arrangements for local transportation. At the advertised time of departure the plane had not yet left London.

In the days of Imperial Airways I used to have to go to Paris frequently on business. I always went comfortably by the Golden Arrow and on many occasions I have been waiting on the airfields at Le Bourget, or Croydon, to meet colleagues who came by air. Even though the distance between London and Nice is roughly four times greater than from London to Paris, it is still frequently quicker to travel by train because, especially between November and March, a calendar is more useful than a watch to time arrivals.

It had been some while since Esmé and I had managed to have a private talk, so we availed ourselves of the drive back to Ste Monique. 'I expect you want to know what's what between me and János,' she began.

'Not unless you feel like telling me,' I replied.

'I'd like to tell you,' she said reprovingly, 'because I'd like your advice.'

'That is what your father used to say when he was contemplating some piece of transcendental folly. . . .'

'Was he really such a bloody fool as I've often been tempted to believe?'

'Your father was a clever, highly intelligent, unwise man with a tendency to go off half-cocked. He was a man who carried a little devil on his shoulder, constantly whispering bad advice to him. Confucius was thinking of men like him when he warned against the perils of cleverness without

89

wisdom. But anyway, let's leave your father out of this. . . .'

'You started it.'

'I know I did, because you constantly remind me of him. What particular kind of advice of mine would you like to ignore?'

'You bastard!'

'Thank you.'

'It's about János and his system. I'm satisfied now that his big ugly nose—did you ever see such a squashed, misshapen one?—really can smell out the winners and losers, if not all the time, often enough for us to make a clean-up. What do you think?'

'Against all the probabilities, I'm inclined to agree with you,' I told her. 'By the way you speak of "us" I imagine János wants you to go in with him. Is that it?'

She nodded. 'I know it's taking a chance, Steve, but I don't seem to have much choice in the matter. I've got no money. Mother won't help me and Pedro can't, or won't, which is much the same thing, and I know it's a waste of time trying to get any out of a mean bastard like you. I don't fancy sleeping with strangers, so what's a girl to do? Whenever I approach a man with the idea of getting a job, sooner or later it comes round to bed work. Well, as you know, János and I have got over all that. I expect, of course, if we go into this together seriously, we shall pop into bed from time to time. It would be the normal, friendly thing to do, but there would be no conditions about it. If and when I'm screwed it will be because I want to be screwed and for no other reason. . . .

'Any other arrangement, when you come to think of it, wouldn't work. I wouldn't care for it if János had another girl-friend on the side and I don't expect he'd like me to have a boy-friend, so unless I'm to live the life of a cloistered nun and he that of a Trappist monk, which wouldn't suit either of us, we are the logical people to satisfy each other's urges. Can you find fault with that?'

'I didn't know that you were such an incurable romantic, Esmé. No, seeing things as you evidently see them, I can find no fault with it ... as far as it goes. But, aside from the possibility of making a lot of money, there doesn't seem to be much future in it. Shall we say you can spend five years racketing about gambling hells before you wear out your welcome. What then? You'll be no bargain then. The bloom will have gone off the peach. Even if you can survive as much as five years of it, you must admit that it's a pretty shabby way of earning a living and, never doubt it, some of the shabbiness will rub off on you.

'Even if it is an old-fashioned word and concept, you were born a lady, Esmé. Ask yourself how long you would remain one.'

'Being a lady is a luxury I can't afford any more, Steve,' she said, with a catch in her voice.

We drove the rest of the way home in silence.

10

In a village like Ste Monique virtually nothing is private.
Thus it came to my ears that Esmé, after being closeted with
Father Delorme for more than an hour, went off to find
János, returning with him. The pair of them then spent
another hour with the old priest. As neither of them
mentioned this to me, I felt bound to behave as though I
knew nothing of it.

However lightly given, the fact was that I *had* given
some sort of assurance to her father that I would keep an eye
on her. In this I had failed and the failure rankled with me.
I asked myself repeatedly what else I could have done. To have
given her money would have been fatuous. She would have
spent it in record time and found herself in exactly the same
position as before. Nothing short of making her an allowance
indefinitely would serve, and the value of this was doubtful.
When her father held the purse-strings he could not control
her. Why should I hope to succeed where he had failed?
Besides, I didn't want to control her, or waste time trying.
The Esmés of this world are influenced by advice as much
as a steamroller is influenced by an insect.

When I encountered Father Delorme later on, it was not
hard to guess that the interviews had been thunderous. The
way he looked at me through narrowed eyes told me that he
regarded me as being largely responsible for Esmé's fall from
grace. We chatted uneasily of this and that, of anything in
fact but that which had caused his mood. 'As you do not
appear to like me today,' I said after ten minutes or so, 'I
will go home and read a book in the garden.'

At dinner that evening Esmé had very little to say. Over
the coffee she announced that she and János were leaving
for London a couple of days thence.

'You've got lovely weather for it,' I said, or something equally idiotic. The atmosphere was a little strained between us. I think she was waiting for me to ask what was wrong. After a long silence she said : 'That old priest has a dirty tongue. If any other man had spoken to me in the way he did, I'd have slapped his face.'

I remained silent.

'He told us to our faces,' she went on, 'that we behaved like farmyard animals. How dared he!'

'What did you expect?' I asked. 'A pat on the back for your courage in defying the conventions. You're the practising Christian. I'm not. You went to see the old man voluntarily, didn't you? Nobody dragged you there, so I imagine you went there for comfort, advice or something of that kind. You indulge in plenty of plain speaking yourself, so why deny a priest the same privilege? In fact, why go to see him at all if all you want is to have your follies rubber-stamped?'

'Don't sound so bloody unctuous when you've got your tongue in your cheek.'

'But I haven't got my tongue in my cheek. I'm completely serious. I don't go to Father Delorme for comfort, advice, forgiveness, or anything else that priests are supposed to have on tap. I go because I like him and his intelligent conversation. But, I assure you, if I ever weaken and go to him for the things which the *croyants* seek, I won't be offended because he speaks plainly, or fails to tell me what I want to hear. If you're a Christian, then behave like one. If you're not, then don't let yourself be cornered by a priest. It's perfectly simple and I don't have to apologize to *you* for the vulgarism . . . pee or get off the pot.'

I expected her to start throwing things then, but she began to laugh and we were soon friends again.

The next morning when we were having elevenses in the garden, she harped again indignantly on being accused of animal behaviour.

'Look over there,' I said, 'and you may discover that Father Delorme was paying you a compliment.'

93

I have two dachshund bitches. With all the disadvantages, I prefer them to males. These two are old friends, mother and daughter. The mother was aged fifteen, the daughter aged eight or nine. They have never been separated. Even when they have had pups they shared them, for they are both born mothers. They seem to love anything young ... except human children. The presence of a litter of kittens causes them to drip milk everywhere.

It is years since I made mention in a book of these dogs because the droolings of some writers as they relate nauseatingly false anecdotes on the subject offend me deeply. When I come across it, I close the book and give it away.

The fifteen-year-old mother had lost nearly all her teeth, and those she had wobbled precariously. She and her daughter shared a passion for hazelnuts, which for years they have eaten in prodigious quantities. Esmé and I watched, fascinated, as the old lady tried vainly to crack the nuts. When with a sigh she had given up the attempt, the daughter cracked more than a dozen, leaving them for her mother to eat. Then, and only then, the daughter began to crack and eat some herself.

'I'm prepared to bet that you never forget that,' I said.

'I feel better now.'

When János arrived to pick up Esmé and her baggage, I watched them drive away with mixed feelings. The mixed feelings were mine. I don't know what they felt, if anything. House guests are a strain, even the best and most considerate of them. They have a way, without meaning to, of bringing their problems with them and because these, like most problems, are insoluble except in terms of time, they leave a disturbing residue behind them when they go. For days I could not see Esmé's place at table, or the easy chair she favoured in the living-room, without being conscious of her unsolved problems.

Healthy rebellion is a fine thing. Every great reform in history has been sponsored by rebels. Although by nature I am not a conformist or a slave to the conventions, I still believe that there is a case for them. Where Esmé and her

94

father went adrift was in behaving as though all conventions were always wrong. Instead of obeying instinctively like sheep, they disobeyed instinctively and, therefore, without thought. Marriage, although often given pontifical names, is a convention. Without wishing to start a hare, I would say that women have more to thank marriage for than men. I hated to see Esmé being so reckless with her life. A time might well come when she wanted passionately to have a home, husband and children, only to find that she had missed the bus.

* * * *

I can never think of an evening at a casino as a social occasion. I don't mind dining at a casino with friends, but once in the gaming rooms, I am on my own. I don't like being watched. When, after a lapse of some months, I went off one evening on the spur of the moment to indulge in my small and harmless gambling, it annoyed me to observe that I was being dogged and my bets noted by a casino employee.

At the bar, where I went after cashing in my chips, determined not to play any more, Chartrain paused politely enough to pass the time of day with me.

'Has the roulette wheel been kind to you?' he asked amiably.

'I expect when you return to your office you will find on your desk a complete record of every stake I made, compiled by your diligent employee . . . the one with acne.' I said this somewhat acidly.

Chartrain did not trouble to deny that I had been watched, although he did not admit it in so many words.

'You know, Monsieur Chartrain,' I went on, 'you do me too much honour, for the scale of my play does not warrant such flattering attention. All the same, I prefer to be without it. . . .'

'I have not seen the so charming Madame Latta for some time. She is well, I trust. . . ?'

'On the last occasion when I saw her she was very well. . . .'

'And Monsieur Tisza also, I hope?'

95

'In splendid health also, thank you. If they ever return to the Côte d'Azur I will tell them of your kind interest.'

'Please do so, monsieur, and'—he added as an afterthought —'I will make enquiries about the employee who has caused you annoyance. Be assured it will not occur again.'

Without being so impolite as to say so, what he said meant pretty plainly that if you keep the wrong company you mustn't be surprised if you are tarred with the same brush.

I did not know how much János with his various stooges had won from the casino, but for it to have aroused such interest it must have been fairly substantial. I was sure, too, that János lurking in the Baccara Bar while others played the system he had invented, had not escaped notice. I am certain as I can be that every stake made had been noted and subjected to analysis by the casino's tame system hound, who must have been baffled by the realization that there was no system. My guess would be that several croupiers and other employees had come under suspicion of being in cahoots with János, Esmé or both.

If Esmé ever came to stay with me again, I would make it a condition that she should keep out of the casinos on the coast.

'*Sans indiscretion,*' said Chartrain on my next visit, 'is it your considered opinion that this young Hungarian has succeeded, where nobody else has, and that he has invented some clever way of winning?'

'It would be idle to deny that some such thought has been in my mind,' I replied cagily. 'But like you, I have watched his play. I have even on two or three occasions taken his advice and won money doing it. I am sure that you are well informed in detail about this. But an infallible system, like you I do not admit the possibility. No, such things do not happen. Nevertheless, I grant you that Monsieur Tisza is a remarkably clever young man. I go further. If anyone ever does come up with an infallible system, don't be surprised if he is a Hungarian.'

Amiability restored, we left it at that. Nor was I being entirely facetious.

Once upon a time I possessed what was known on the China Coast as a three-piece dollar, a silver Mexican dollar worth about two shillings at the time, which had been split into two circular discs. About sixty per cent of the silver had been scooped out, leaving only two thin shells and both sides of the coin intact. Then someone had filled the hollow spaces with some base metal, joined the two pieces together, re-made the flanged circumference, reconstituting it as an apparently untouched dollar. The profit on this laborious and ingenious work had been rather less than a shilling. It was done entirely by a very rich man for his own amusement. It rang like a good coin. Why did he do it? That was the question I asked. It was, I learned, a spare-time amusement. He made several such three-piece dollars every year, putting some back into circulation, or giving the odd one to friends as a souvenir. The satisfaction was in outsmarting the clever boys who controlled the coinage, the eagle-eyed shroffs at the banks and the long succession of people through whose hands these devalued coins would pass as genuine.

This rich merchant had in his veins some of the same blood which crossed Asia and a large part of Europe with Genghis Khan and his mounted horde which foundered and was turned back on the plains of Hungary, but not before they had sowed their seed there.

It is from this legacy of oriental blood, I believe, that the Hungarians still derive their ingenuity and the spiritual need to outsmart others. The János system of smelling out winners was his particular form of three-piece dollar. Not being a rich man, he had to do it professionally rather than as a hobby, but I am persuaded that the naughty little boy hidden under that rich Chinese merchant's rolls of fat was the mainspring which made János tick. There were no horses on his immediate horizon so, perforce, he could not be a horse-coper.

This may not be precisely and in detail a correct analysis, indeed almost certainly it is not, but I don't believe it strays very far from the real János. There was nothing dishonest about his system. He broke no rules, written or unwritten. There was no marking of cards, interfering with the balance of the roulette wheel, or other jiggery-pokery employed by tricksters. He was doing openly what nobody believed was possible and, therefore, had no need to take precautions. To me the worst aspect was that it killed all the fun of gambling, turning glorious uncertainty into dull, pedestrian certainty with as much glamour about it as the compound interest table. Always provided, that is, that the system was nothing more than a long, inexplicable run of luck. I did not believe this was so, but I could not close my mind to the possibility.

II

Over a period of many weeks, with several house guests whom
I have not troubled to mention, and a constant stream of
visitors for lunch or dinner, I had tended to lose touch with
local events. I would be very happy to lose touch altogether
with most local events which, with the passing of time, have
lost all novelty. Maybe it is wrong of me, but I just can't get
excited because the roof of the *Mairie* leaks. It is a matter of
complete indifference to me whether, or not, the mooted
Ste Monique Wine Festival ever materializes, if only because
the only locally grown wine that is fit to drink is almost never
offered for sale. The white wines taste as though the horse
should have been taken to the vet, while the red are thin and
vinegary. I grow a little red wine which, one year in three,
is surprisingly good, but I earn an undeserved reputation for
generosity by giving the other two years' crop to the old
people of the village.

When Father Delorme said somewhat acidly that I should
take more interest in local affairs, I knew from long
experience that it was the prelude to something unpleasant,
or something which would cost me money. I waited for it.

'I consider it is your duty to do something about this
crowd of your unruly compatriots who have descended on us
like a plague of locusts.'

'What compatriots, ruly or unruly?' I demanded to know.

'The popular term for them, I believe, is "hippies". Do
you know what that means?'

'I am not sure,' I replied, 'but I gather that if you have
a lot of hair on view, never wash, never work, beg what you
can and steal what you cannot, you qualify as a hippy. But I
overlook the most important qualification: if you are male
you must look like a dirty and degenerate female, and con-

versely. What the word hippy means I do not know and on the whole would prefer not to know. I have seen quite a few people answering to that description in and around the village. Now you propose that I—why me?—should do something about it. Do precisely what?'

'Persuade them to behave themselves better or, best of all, go somewhere else. They are not welcome here and the temper of the village is such as may well lead to violence.'

'Seriously, Father, what specifically have they done?'

'I myself have seen them copulating on the beach with admiring children as spectators. I am told that they defecate wherever they may happen to be when the urge takes them. Is that enough?'

While I do not consider myself obliged in any way to take up the cudgels on behalf of ill-behaved fellow countrymen, I don't like any wholesale condemnation of them without knowledge of the facts. Although it did not occur to me to impugn Father Delorme as an eye-witness, his first-hand knowledge of copulation cannot on the face of things have been great. But even if he had not been mistaken, his keen, priestly eye could not very well have determined their nationality unless they wore Union Jacks sewn into their underwear . . . if they wore underwear.

I made it my business to ascertain the facts.

As nothing ever happened in the village to which my old friend Lentrua was not privy, I addressed myself to him. I found him smouldering with rage because those of the hippies who had any money used his bar as a meeting place, keeping out the kind of customers he wanted.

'Why do you not refuse to serve them?' I asked. 'You do not have to serve them.'

'On the contrary, my friend, I risk losing my licence if I do not. They know that as well as I do, and while on these premises they have not behaved so badly that I would be justified in ejecting them.'

While Lentrua and I were talking I had a copy of an English newspaper tucked under my arm, identifying me with reasonable certainty as British.

100

Two hippies detached themselves from the group at the end of the bar and approached me. Would I buy them a drink? Yes, in exchange for some information, I would.

'How many of you are there?' I asked.

'Somewhere about sixty ... perhaps a few more,' one of them replied in the tones of an educated man.

'Are you all British?'

'Are you crazy, man? Only five of us are British.'

'What are the rest?'

'A few French ... maybe a dozen, no more. Some Arabs, maybe twenty Yugo-Slavs and some Dutch. Yes, there's one or two Americans. Why do you want to know?'

'I've been told that you were all British and I was going to tell you, in case you don't know it already, that feeling in the village is running high against you.'

'So what?'

'So, if you know what's good for you, you'll move on.'

'You threatening us?'

'No, but I'm telling you that the people here are in an ugly mood and, unless you're looking for trouble, in which case you'll get it, you'd be wise to think about moving. That's all.'

'What's it to you whether we go or stay?'

'Nothing at all ... now that I know that you are not all British. You see, I live here. I can now let it be known that only five of you are British.'

Father Delorme, not best pleased at having been caught out, would not give ground. 'Even if these dirty ruffians are not all British,' he said sourly, 'I imagine you will not deny that the disease entered France from England. After all, the Channel is not very wide and it would be surprising if a few Frenchmen had not been contaminated.'

'Would you like me to write a list of the unpleasant things we've caught from France over the years?' I asked, matching his tone and leaving him before he could think up a good retort.

Nevertheless, I find myself wishing that all the cranks, oddities, perverts and other peculiar people on the Riviera were not so freely labelled British. Particularly so because there are enough of them sometimes to make it appear so.

*   *   *   *

After perhaps a couple of months without word from Esmé, I fell back on the old bromide that no news is good news and, strangely, for I had been expecting the worst, so it turned out to be. Her letter when it came was written on the notepaper of one of London's very expensive West-end hotels.

Esmé writes as she lives. Her handwriting sprawls. She favours purple ink and exclamation marks. Her letter occupied seventeen sheets of paper and was insufficiently stamped. As I cannot improve on it, I quote it verbatim:

Dear Steve: Did I write you a bread-and-butter letter to thank you for putting up with me for so long? If not, consider yourself thanked now.

As you can see from the address, all goes well with us ... anyway financially. The thieving bastards soak us £25 per day for this suite, plus and plus and plus. But, with the János system getting into its stride, it is a mere trifle.

János has abandoned the idea of smelling strangers. He says the men all reek of whisky and not so good cigars, while the women give off gin and synthetic perfumes which kill the subtler odours he requires. Instead, he smells me. When I smell like a winner, I go to one of the clubs to gamble. When I smell like a loser, which has been quite often, we don't gamble. We tried the experiment on my losing nights of having me to go to the tables and lose small sums, while János opposed me for fairly large sums. But for reasons we don't understand, it didn't work. János believes, and he could be right, that as we are partners our luck is in some way joint and intermingled and, therefore, cannot be separated. It is a weird and wonderful theory, but I am half sold on it. János is a queer mixture with a twisted mind and wonderfully clear vision. I am sure that he would have succeeded at anything he put his hand to. You will understand, I think, that his talents are being wasted shamefully this way. But oh, how the money rolls in!

We have joined six gambling clubs in or near London so

as not to become too well known. They are sleazy places for the most part. Even at the better ones the men seem to be prosperous shits, while the women are overdressed and loud. It seems to be generally accepted that American Mafia types are the behind-the-scenes owners. As long as they don't bring in machine-guns, I don't care. The men in control give me the willies. They are too suave. I think they shave three times daily. They smile too readily, like babies with wind, but there is no warmth in their utterly reptilian eyes. We are thinking of going into the provinces, Manchester and places like that. But so far I don't think we have attracted any attention.

One of the snags we are up against is that, being foreigners, we cannot open a banking account with the loot. We can only pay into a bank money which originates abroad. We have temporarily rented a safe deposit box. What happens when we want to take the loot out of this country?

Donald has begun divorce proceedings. I didn't think he would. I am glad. He is a shocking bore, but he has not blotted his copybook and it wouldn't be fair on him to bear the onus of it all.

I shall not marry János, whatever happens. I like him. He is good in bed. But there is no fun in him and he is too purposeful.

All seems plain sailing, but I have a hunch that it will blow up. If this happens and if I promise to behave, will you welcome me with open arms?

Love,
Esmé

P.S. Can you advise us about the money question?

In my reply to this letter I made only a very brief reference to their money difficulties: 'Matters touching on your postscript are better not put in writing.'

Like everyone else living out of the U.K. I know a dozen ways of getting money out of the country. It is and has been since 1946 simplicity itself. That I have not done it is because I have not had to do it. Mine passes legally. Esmé and János would have to solve that difficulty without my help.

Now that Esmé and János were away from the coast my

relations with Chartrain improved, helped doubtless by the fact that I lost on four or five consecutive visits to the casino. The amounts involved were small, never more than my maximum of 500 francs. But, as people are so fond of saying, it was the principle of the thing. The fact of losing suggested that I was not able to nudge Fortune by any unorthodox means.

With this shadow out of the way, we were able to chat amiably about many things. One evening he told me that the Riviera Casino and others were losing trained staff to the London gambling clubs, which were able to offer greater inducements. 'I think your people are being very short-sighted,' I told him. 'There may well come a revulsion of feeling against organized gambling in England. There is already a bad smell. It only needs a big scandal to kill it. Then where would your ex-employees be?'

'Would you say that these clubs are well conducted?' Chartrain asked me.

'I have no first-hand knowledge of them,' I told him, 'and I have been given such conflicting reports that I do not know what to believe.'

'I intend to go to England shortly to find out for myself,' he said. 'I like England and have many English friends. That is my chief reason for going. The other is mere curiosity.'

It seemed the friendly thing to do to warn Esmé that she and János might well run into Chartrain at one of the clubs. If they did he would surely recognize them. It was anybody's guess whether he might feel obliged to tip off the owners to the fact that they were harbouring serpents unawares.

I might have spared myself the trouble. A few days before Chartrain went to England the damage was already done.

* * * *

The first intimation of Esmé's imminent arrival came in a phone call from Paris. 'You're very welcome,' I told her, 'but don't expect me to meet you at Nice airport.'

'Don't worry. I'm coming by car.'

Then came another call from Aix-en-Provence early one morning to say that if convenient she would arrive before lunch. She duly arrived in a spanking new British car which had cost her not less than £3,000. 'Have you got a safe place for this?' was her first question. 'This' was a smallish crocodile suitcase with gold fittings. Carried over her arm was a nasty putty-coloured fur coat which, I expect, was also expensive.

What's in it?' I asked, taking the case from her.

'Boodle.'

'How much boodle?'

'It must be somewhere around twelve thousand quid.'

In those minutes I discovered the chief reason why I tolerated Esmé and her frequently outrageous behaviour. It was that she scorned to lie, or dissemble, never indulged in the English vice of giving ugly things pretty names and never sought to attribute to herself motives any higher than they really were. Like her father, there wasn't a mean streak in her, nor room for pettiness.

'While I'm locking the case in a filing cabinet . . . it won't go into my safe . . . you get yourself washed and join me for a drink. We'll talk about what to do with it later.'

Alphonsine is the only French cook I have ever known, or heard of, who knows how to make a curry. As served in France it is usually a boiled chicken over which someone has poured some pale yellow, tasteless slop from which, if one is lucky, there comes a very faint aroma of curry. For years, about once monthly, I used to make my own curries. Alphonsine used to turn up her nose, make gagging sounds and sulk somewhere else. Then one day, when two guests had defected, there was a lot of chicken curry left over. I went into the kitchen after lunch to tell her not to throw it away as curry was one of the few dishes better warmed up. To my astonishment I caught her in the act of guzzling it with every sign of relish. She was trapped.

In turn I taught her how to make vegetable, egg, prawn, mutton and chicken curries, each of which calls for entirely

105

different methods. Now on curry days she eats far more than I do, a sincere tribute to a once-detested dish.

On the day of Esmé's arrival there was a medium to hot mutton curry, with poppadums, grated coconut, Bombay duck and real mango chutney, this last not the chutney of commerce, but the genuine article with thick slices of turpentiney mango and hot condiments. I buy it by the case from Madras.

Esmé loves a curry, the hotter the better. She was brought up on hellfire sauces in Central America.

We ate in almost unbroken silence. It was a joy to see the ecstatic look on Esmé's face as she did it justice. Few women I have ever known have eaten with such undisguised gusto. Alphonsine was shocked by the small amount which left the table.

'That,' said Esmé with a deep sigh, 'was the first meal I have enjoyed for five months.'

'You astound me,' I said. 'While most London restaurant food, admittedly, is abominable, there are still a few places which are above reproach. From all accounts you could have afforded the best.'

'Not with that bastard János watching every mouthful,' she said bitterly. 'He wouldn't let me eat anything but bland food. No soups. Steamed or boiled fish. Very little meat of any kind. No condiments. No coffee, weak tea. Bread and butter *ad lib*. No alcohol, of course. It nearly killed me.'

'I assure you that you look well on it,' I said. 'But since when has János become a doctor, or dietician?'

'He didn't give a bugger about my health. All he was concerned with was my smell.

'I had to cut out smoking, too. I cheated once and had some anchovy toast for tea. I didn't think he'd notice it, but would you believe it, the bugger not only noticed it but said I smelled like a kipper curing shed. All scent was barred, of course. Life was hardly worth living.'

'It certainly doesn't sound very exciting,' I was forced to agree. 'But the fact that it worked was surely some compensation?'

106

'Steve, you may believe me, that bloody János is inhuman. The last straw which would have broken this camel's back, if other events hadn't intervened, was in the matter of sex. "You'll have to get your mind off sex," he said as primly as a Sunday school teacher. "I can't smell anything but sex."

' "Well," I told him, "that makes us square because I can't think of anything but sex." I was so randy my teeth were chattering. But was he interested? No, he was not interested. All he wanted to know was whether my smell was right for the evening's play. Then I lost my temper and walked out of the suite. From a downstairs phone I rang an old boy-friend of mine. He was in, luckily. When I returned to the hotel around five o'clock the next morning I was feeling better. But János wasn't. In fact, he was bloody rude.'

'And although you were evidently coining money,' I said, 'you allowed a little thing like that to throw it all up?'

'A little thing like that!' she yelled. 'You may call it that but I don't. When you men want what you call a piece of tail you go off and get it. It's all right because you are men. But when a girl feels the same way ... oh no, that's different. Well, it isn't different and I'll bet the most respectable of the Victorian women would, when they felt that way, sling the embroidery at the aspidistra and nip out for a bit of slap and tickle. Don't you believe the contrary. They'd have blown their gaskets otherwise.'

Esmé never left the smallest loophole for misunderstanding.

'If you insist,' I said, 'I will withdraw the words "little thing like that", and substitute "big thing like that". But little or big, are you going to allow it to break up this most profitable partnership?'

'No, that wasn't really what caused us to pack up in England. What really happened was that one evening, just as I was leaving the tables, a smarmy voice said: "Good evening Madame Latta. London's gain is our loss. I trust you are well." I recognized him at once, although I don't know his name. He was one of the chaps who strolled around

107

the gaming rooms at the Riviera Casino keeping an eye on the croupiers and the players.

'I need hardly tell you that when János and I arrived the next evening, it was only to find that our admission cards had been withdrawn. We knew it would be a waste of time going to the other clubs, so I went over to Paris and ... well, here I am.'

'And János, where's he?'

'In Vienna, working some fiddle to get relatives out of Hungary.'

'It sounds very noble and praiseworthy.'

'Funnily enough, I rather think it is. He's a funny cuss is our János. He won't forget that the Hungary he knew doesn't exist any more, and in his secret heart of hearts I think he dreams of going back there some day.'

'And in the meantime?'

'When he runs out of money, or just wants more, I expect we'll team up again in some other part of the world. He knows I'm here and I shall hear from him. You see, he knows when he's well off, and he knows that I don't cheat where money is concerned. That, you see, is one of the weak spots in the János system: he must have a partner. He can't smell his own luck ... that's what it amounts to....

'You know, Steve,' she went on, her voice taking on a whine, 'if getting hold of some money wasn't so important to me I'd be tempted to drop the whole thing and cut clean. Here, away from János's influence and in the cold light of reason, I know the whole thing is nonsense. Luck ... good or bad ... doesn't, can't have a smell, and I tell myself that only the corkscrew mind of a Hungarian could believe the contrary. You feel much the same way as I do, don't you, Steve? You don't accept it altogether....'

'I suppose I don't accept it altogether because I don't have to accept it, or reject it. I'm an outsider who's seen a little of the János system in operation, whereas you're in it ... up to the neck. I'm just about as neutral in the matter as it's possible to be. We live in an age of new marvels or, perhaps it would be more accurate to say,

108

old marvels revamped. As an example, computers. Our grandfathers would have laughed at the idea although, as we know now, the computer is in fact only a tarted up abacus, which has been performing prodigies of calculation for several thousand years.

'Then along comes János with his proposition which, if you think of the matter, is no more improbable today than the computer was a hundred years ago. I was reading only yesterday a comparison of human and animal senses of smell.* Of the sense of smell of a German sheep-dog, the author says that readings of an instrument called an olfactometer suggest that this dog's sense of smell is one million times better than the human. Some humans have a better sense of smell than others, as we know. It is a matter of degree. Nature being full of freaks, or sports, isn't it just possible that János is one and that his nose has recaptured the olfactory perception which we lost somewhere down the labyrinthine ways of evolution?'

* *The Magic of the Senses*, by Vitus B. Droscher, W. H. Allen, London.

In the cold, wet weather which comes to the Côte d'Azur, as it does for some weeks at any time between November and March, I would just as soon be in one of the dripping suburbs of Manchester. It is depressing in a way that no other place I know is depressing. Landscapes which in pale golden winter sunshine look as if they had been dipped in honey assume leaden hues. Olives and pines cease to be green, or to give the illusion of being green, becoming instead a grey which seems to absorb all the light.

Esmé had gone off somewhere down the coast in her expensive new car and would be back when it suited her. Alphonsine, probably for the same reason as I was, was in a foul temper, muttering in her beard about lack of appreciation and going somewhere where she would be appreciated. In an effort to be helpful I offered to drive her to the railway station.

Father Delorme, in whose company I can usually find amusement, wasn't being very friendly. A day or so previously we had brawled about Papal Infallibility, a subject on which I find it impossible to talk reasonably. His sister—Father Delorme's sister, that is, not the Pope's—with whom I have barely been on speaking terms for several years, snarled at me with the accusation that I was trying to kill her brother by over-exciting him.

Life was extremely dull. Even that slanderous old hag Lady Baskerville had been polite to me when we met the previous day at the house of a mutual acquaintance. It had been a great disappointment because I was ready for her and compelled to smother some of the flowers of speech which hovered on my lips. It is a part of my religion never to be the aggressor. Old women who are polite to me—even those who are not actively impolite—can be assured of politeness from me. Lady B. knows that. I think she now knows the limits of my chivalry, perhaps because she knows I do not possess a horse. Denied even the stimulus of a brawl with my *bête noire*, I went down into the village to visit my old friend Lentrua at his bar.

I have known Lentrua for almost exactly half my life. He is a paradoxical figure who uses a viperous tongue to conceal the fact that he has a warm heart. I find that almost without exception we see people and situations through the same faintly jaundiced eyes.

The bar was empty. Windows in the village were curtained. People who put their cats out slammed home the bolts of their doors with a finality which suggested that they were going to spend the evening goggling at the inanities of their magic lanterns and addling what little remained of their grey matter.

'Why,' asked Lentrua, when we were settled down with our drinks, 'are you English such idiots as to want to put yourselves in the death trap of the Common Market?'

'The answer to that,' I replied, 'is that the English ... British people are idiots, *bien entendu,* but not such idiots as to want that. . . .'

'Then why do you state your determination to enter?'

'We don't. Our abominable politicians do it without consulting us. . . .'

'But you elected them to power in order to enter the Common Market, did you not?'

'No, we did nothing of the kind. Under what we British call our democratic system the British people are never allowed to vote on any important issue. Our politicians make alliances, declare war, nationalize vast industries, all without reference to the wishes of the people.'

'They sound as bad as ours. But do they not know that with your high wages you cannot compete with Common Market countries, to say nothing of the Boches who work like moles.'

'Of course they know it,' I was forced to tell him, 'but

111

politicians, not only ours, don't care whether they ruin the country so long as the Party survives. In our case the Conservative Party is financed by Big Business. We are creeping up towards the million unemployed, but that isn't enough. I have heard more than one of these boys talk nostalgically of the Great Depression, that wonderful legendary time when the working man was reduced to such desperate straits that he was docile and glad to work for any wages which would enable him and his family to eat. The Common Market is the stick by which Big Business hopes to beat the people into submission. . . .'

'But will that not ruin Big Business too?'

'Not at all. If Britain is a member of the Common Market British industries can be transferred to, say, Calabria or Sicily, where labour is cheap. What is to stop it?'

'I do not understand it,' said Lentrua, shaking his head.

'Nor do the British people . . . yet. But they will . . . when it is too late.'

We wore that out. Then it became apparent that Lentrua had something on his mind. 'It is being freely said in the village,' he began, 'that the young Hungarian who sometimes stays with the Belgian family at *La Tour du Moulin* has invented a gambling system which is going to ruin all the casinos. He and the young lady who is the daughter of your old friend. Is there any truth in the matter, do you think? Only a week ago at this bar I was told it by Cassini whose brother is a croupier at the Riviera Casino. He should know.'

'If anyone had invented such a thing as an infallible system, the casinos would have closed down already,' I hedged. Lentrua is a friend and I do not like to lie to friends. 'Nevertheless, to try to answer your question, this young man has, I believe, won considerable sums of money. But this was some while ago and to the best of my knowledge it is many months since he has been on the coast.'

'And the young lady who is staying at your house, does she speak of the matter? I ask because, according to Cassini, they played as partners.'

'Yes, she has spoken of the matter often. I think she won

112

some money, but she has never said that she, or the Hungarian, had an infallible system. He may think so, of course, but as you may know without my telling you, Hungarians are not quite like other people.'

'I have never, as far as I know, spoken to a Hungarian.'

'Then, let me tell you, you have missed a rich experience. . . .'

'If he has invented this infallible system,' said Lentrua, thoughtfully, 'you are in a good position to know, being friends with them both. I have never been in a casino,' he went on with a faraway look in his eyes, 'but it would be a fine thing to be able to win as much money as one liked. No more having to be polite to drunken bores! No more having to refuse credit to people who would not pay even if I were fool enough to let them have it! No more loud, red-necked German tourists who buy one beer and think they own the place. Of all the smells I detest it is that of aniseed, yet three out of every five drinks I serve are *pastis*. They breathe it all over me. Although I use turpentine to kill it, the bar reeks of it. It is everywhere and there is no escape from it.'

'What would you do if you had this infallible system?' I asked. 'First I would empty every bottle of *pastis* into the *pissoir*. Then I would employ all the old women to scrub away the smell of it. Then I would sell my licence and, until the new owner took over, I would invite all my friends to help me drink the stock of everything down to the last bottle. . . .'

'What if they wanted *pastis*?'

'No man who drinks *pastis* is a friend of mine!' He was so intense that I could not help laughing. 'You have the air of one who knows more than he says,' Lentrua went on, 'so if you ever get to learn about this system, it would be a friendly act to let me into the secret.'

Even that I wonder. My experience is that a lot of easy money does far more harm than good. We tend to value money by the sweat we expend to buy it. When it arrives like manna from heaven and without sweat all our values are turned upside down. Only mugs work hard.

113

Passing Lentrua's bar some days later, he came to the door and beckoned me in. 'Is the name of the lady who stays with you Madame Latta?' he asked. I nodded affirmatively. 'Then there are two men in the village asking for her. They were here an hour ago enquiring about her.'

'What sort of men?'

'It is hard to say,' he replied. 'They were talking English but their clothes were not English. Hard types both of them.'

I thanked him and went on my way. If two men wanted to talk to Esmé it would not take them long to find her, but it didn't follow that she wanted to talk to them.

In the hall I keep a writing pad and a ballpoint pen. It is for chance callers to write down their names and business in case they speak no French, Alphonsine's only language. The pad is one I think I must have pinched from a government office years ago. It asks for the caller's name, address, telephone number and nature of business. For reasons I have never understood, most callers are fiercely reluctant to use it. I warned Alphonsine that there might be callers.

The mistral was blowing that day, so after lunch Esmé and I drank our coffee in a sheltered part of the garden below wind level. We heard the front door-bell ring, but as Alphonsine did not appear I assumed the caller was for her. Ten minutes must have elapsed before she arrived looking as flustered as a wet hen. Across one of the forms, which she held in her hand, was the word 'private' against 'nature of business'. No name, address or phone number. 'There are two men,' she said. 'They want to see mademoiselle.'

As I could not expect Alphonsine to deal with the situation unaided, I went into the house by a rear entrance to see and, if necessary, eject the callers. When I reached the front entrance, they were not there, so I returned to Esmé. I might have spared myself any anxiety on her account, for she seemed well able to cope with the situation unaided. One of the men was a Spanish type, probably Latin-American. As I arrived on the scene she was holding forth in Spanish. The only words I could be sure of were '*hijo de puta.*' She then whirled on the other who, presumably, spoke English. 'In case you don't know what a *hijo de puta* is, look in a mirror and you will see one. Who the hell do you think you are busting uninvited into a private garden and refusing to give your name! Ashamed of it, I suppose. . . .'

'Lady,' the wretched man said, 'if you'll only give me the chance I'll tell you anything you want to know. I have a letter here that explains everything. . . .'

'Then put it in the post and get the hell out of here.'

'You heard,' I said, thinking it was time I did something, 'so on your way.'

Reluctantly they went.

'What did they want?' I asked.

'It must have been to do with the gambling,' she replied.

'What else could be of interest to plug-uglies like that? I've seen the Cuban somewhere else. It'll come to me.'

'Something to do with the János system?'

'Bound to be . . . unless they are recruiting agents for a whorehouse. Or maybe they want me to run a stall at a church bazaar.'

'Might it not have been smarter to have found out what they wanted?' I asked. 'By the same token it might have been wiser not to be quite so outspoken. I couldn't have coped with the pair of them and I'm sure you couldn't.'

'The Cuban was the boss man of the two and I coped with him, didn't I? Never give that sort a chance to speak. What if I did call him a son-of-a-bitch? He's been called it so often that he believes it's true.'

I could almost hear Broom, her father, speaking.

Just as blowflies are attracted to decomposing meat, so certain types of men, and women, gather when they pick up the smell of easy money. Too many knew of János and his system. Casino employees on the Côte d'Azur, their counterparts in England and others impossible to guess, knew that the bar had been put up against János and Esmé. As neither of them had been guilty of bad behaviour and they were known to have won money fairly consistently, the wildest stories had doubtless been circulated. The two visitors bore all the outward appearance of easy money boys ... slick, overdressed with pseudo-gangster overtones. That others would come I did not doubt and, likely enough, be not so easy to get rid of.

'A penny for your thoughts,' said Esmé, after a prolonged silence.

'I found myself wishing,' I replied, 'that you would find yourself a steady, hard-boiled husband with a little more fire than Donald has, able to keep you in line and, when necessary, willing to beat the hell out of you. With two or three kids you could work off your surplus energy washing diapers and doing other chores. As you are now you are a tacit invitation to boyos like those two. . . .'

'They don't bother me a bit,' she said lightly.

'I know they don't,' I retorted. 'That's what I'm complaining about. They ought to bother you as they would any normal young woman from a normal decent background.'

'What is normal, I wonder?'

'If you were normal you wouldn't need to ask that. You should try being respectable for a change. . . .'

'Look who's talking!' she jeered. 'Call yourself respectable?'

'No, not altogether, but I have streaks of respectability that have helped to keep me on the rails. As I see it, respectability is a kind of brake and, carrying the analogy a little further, the faster the car the more it needs brakes.'

'It's a thought anyway.'

But it wasn't even a thought for, as a brightly coloured bird skimmed across the garden, she had forgotten it already.

*   *   *   *

On a day when Esmé's car was out of action after a minor collision on the Croisette at Cannes and mine was being serviced in the village, János, quite unexpectedly, phoned from Nice airport to ask one of us to pick him up. I was out for a walk when the call came. Esmé took it and without knowing, or caring, where my car was, told János that I would fetch him because she could not. When I told her that I needed my car because I was lunching with friends in Hyères, she had the gall to ask me to cancel the engagement. 'Let him hire a car,' I said. 'Better still, let the Belgians he is staying with fetch him.'

As soon as the garage had delivered my car, I drove off to Hyères. It was late evening before János made his appearance in Ste Monique, having taken an airport bus to Cannes, train to Fréjus and a hired car onward. The Belgians were out when he arrived so he came on to my house to borrow the money to pay the car driver. Esmé lent him the money for this.

'Why didn't you hire a car for the whole journey?' I asked him.

'Because I didn't have any money.'

'Then why didn't you say so when you spoke to Esmé by phone?'

'I forgot.'

'Anyway, what's happened to the small fortune you won in London?'

'Most of it went in bribes,' he said calmly. 'I managed to get five people out of Hungary. Then there were the fares to Australia. I left some of the money in the safe deposit box in London, but I have to go there to get any of that.'

János was in many ways like Esmé in that nothing he ever did was done in the ordinary or expected way. Bribes apparently running into thousands of pounds, paid presumably to Hungarian frontier officials, evidently seemed all in the day's work to him, for he told us of it in calm, matter-of-fact tones. The family had had no exit permits and, therefore, no passports. It had cost quite a lot to buy passports in Vienna, presumably forged passports.

'We shall have to go to work soon,' he said to Esmé before we talked of other things.

'Where to this time?' asked Esmé.

'The Bahamas, I think. I'm told there's some heavy gambling there.'

His faith that the János system would extricate him

from all his financial worries was most impressive. His attitude was that of a man with an empty pail going to a well without any doubt that he would find water. Esmé shared this quiet certainty and, I confess, I was beginning to. I think it was the sight of the contents of Esmé's crocodile suitcase which was in large measure responsible for my attitude. Its reality was so vividly, startlingly apparent. There, unarguably, was the living testimony to the perceptiveness of János's flat and not very attractive nose. Those fat wads of Bank of England notes had been wrested from predatory hands more accustomed to raking in than paying out money.

They drove off to London three days later. A week after that I had a postcard from Esmé to say that they were leaving on the following day for the Bahamas. No address given. I would hear all the news in Esmé's own sweet time. In the ordinary sense of the word she was not a good correspondent, but when she felt the need of a confidant, as though I were a neighbour on the other side of the garden fence, she wrote long, rambling and often interesting letters.

From Lentrua I learned that the Hungarian System, as it was called in the village, was one of the chief topics of conversation, and greatly exaggerated stories were in circulation about the amounts alleged to have been won on the coast. This did not trouble me in the least except for the fact that I was assumed to be a participant. Once again Father Delorme tackled me about the cost of recasting the cracked church bell.

'Making every allowance for exaggeration,' he said, 'you must have made a large sum of money out of this allegedly infallible system. While I know it is waste of time appealing to you on religious grounds, your sense of civic responsibility should compel you to spend a trifle of your . . . I will not say ill-gotten . . . easily acquired gains on a worthy purpose.'

'I do not know, or care, what is being said about this matter in the village, Father, but if our Hungarian friend has made a fortune, as is said, I was not associated with him and did not participate. Furthermore, while we are on the subject of infallibility, I suggest that you address yourself to your own head office, not to me. If the recasting of the bell is so important, the matter should present no difficulty.'

There followed one of our periodical coolnesses.

As the story of my fabulous winnings went the rounds, it is hardly necessary to add that it lost nothing in the telling. Sundry members of our unwashed artistic colony tried for a 'touch' and appeared quite miffed at their failure, shocked that I did not leap at the chance of becoming a patron of the arts.

Nearing the end of my patience, I went over to Tangier to stay with one of the few, pitifully few English-speaking heterosexuals still living there. I first knew Tangier in 1929, when it was a charming little place. Very few of the Anglo-Saxon colony had more money than was needed to live in modest comfort. Then it became filled with refugees from Hitler who created the international 'hot' money market, parallel with which were the cigarette smugglers who made it their headquarters for this briefly profitable racket. Someone is supposed to have calculated that if every inhabitant of the Tangier International Zone, as it then was, had smoked cigarettes continuously night and day for 180 years, they would have just about consumed one year's importations of cigarettes. It might just as easily have been eighty or 280 years. Now there is to be seen the ugly spectacle of rich buggers giving hospitality to pretty pansy boys, and rich Lesbians likewise entertaining their poor and similarly sexed sisters, the whole forming a tightly closed circle of perversion which has shocked the well-nigh shock-proof Moorish community.

I was not tempted to linger.

On my return to Ste Monique a fat air mail letter from the Bahamas awaited me. It was, of course, from Esmé, who ran out of purple ink half way through addressing it. It read:

Dear Steve: Chicago must be having to do without its gangsters because they are all here. You never saw such a crew in your life, all talking out of the corners of their mouths. They give me the creeps.

119

I don't know which are worse, the people who have organized the gambling, or those who have come to gamble. János and I for once are in agreement that it is making money the hard way. We have made a little. Everything is roughly five times as expensive as it should be. The food is quite revolting and it is as hot as hell. A hurricane has been threatening to arrive for two days. Provided we can get away before it, the best thing to happen would be for it to blow this place out to sea.

From all accounts Las Vegas, where we go tomorrow, isn't much better, if at all. János says that we shall be able to achieve some sort of anonymity there amongst the huge hordes of suckers who are coming and going all the time.

János is too intense to be much fun. He says his nose is getting better all the time. All he thinks of is making a big killing. It can't come any too soon for me. As for me, I long for the peace of your guest bungalow and I drool when I think of Alphonsine's cooking. Kiss her for me right on the tufted wart.

Love,
Esmé

13

My trip to Tangier, Esmé's letter from the Bahamas and another from a friend living on what the Spaniards call the Costa del Sol, brought home to me with depressing vividness that the world has shrunk frighteningly. A generation and a half ago the only overcrowded places in the world, that is to say places where people went for rest or recreation were, broadly speaking, Blackpool, Brighton, Southend, Coney Island. The more sedate spots such as Menton, Interlaken, Lake Como, Cheltenham, Tunbridge Wells, Pau, San Sebastian, Palm Beach and Bermuda were, even at the height of their seasons, havens of peace. Now there are traffic jams in Athens and Beirut, bumper to bumper driving the full length of the Côte d'Azur. Capri, Ibiza, Torremolinos *et al* have become screaming honky-tonks, while people who demand calm and quiet have to find it in remote valleys of the Dolomites, Pyrenees,, Haute Savoie or, better still, in their own back gardens. Factory workers demand music all day, children demand ice cream with jingles, while travel advertisements selling 'Away from it All' fill otherwise quiet spots with the shrill frenzy from which a few people wanted to escape. Noise has become a kind of success symbol while quiet is for cemeteries. Ste Monique has become a honky-tonk from July 14 to September 15, but for the other ten months the decibel output is tolerable.

My homecoming was somewhat marred by a pile of letters waiting attention, including one from Lady Baskerville, who had phoned seven times according to Alphonsine who, acting on my instructions, refused to accept communications from her.

She was on the line when I answered the phone on the day following my return. She barks on the phone. Also, she

121

never phones, writes or calls unless she wants something out of me. 'Why have you not replied to my letter?' she demanded, her voice full of authority. 'Because I have not read it,' I replied mildly. 'Why not?' she barked, asking for it. 'Because, Lady Baskerville, I recognized your handwriting and I have never had any communication whatsoever from you that was not to my disadvantage. Surely, that was a good enough reason?'

There was a crash as she hung up. I won on points. We were deadlocked. As I would not read her letter, or listen to her demands, her only hope was an emissary. I wondered who it would be. I had not long to wait, but if I had been given a hundred guesses I would have guessed wrong.

When I next saw Father Delorme he said: 'I had a call two days ago from a compatriot of yours, a perplexing gentleman with a small military moustache who, I gather, has spent many years in India. I have observed him more than once at the height of our summer clad in a heavy tweed jacket. . . .'

'A convert perhaps?'

'Indeed, no. In his somewhat pedestrian French, yet with an excellent accent far better than your own, he managed to convey to me in a somewhat roundabout fashion that he came as the personal representative of the Archbishop of Canterbury. It seems that His Grace, who I understand is a most estimable cleric, desires to establish here in Ste Monique an Anglican place of worship. In short, funds are required to buy, build or rent premises for this purpose. Your compatriot, most correctly I considered, asked me whether I had any objections. I told him that, on the contrary, I thought the project a most worthy one. He thanked me and, just as he was leaving, suggested that I should signify my support of the project to you. I then pointed out that I had not offered my support, but that the most I had offered was not to oppose. Between ourselves, my friend, I find this procedure strange . . . strange almost to the point of being suspicious. In your opinion would the Archbishop of Canterbury use such an approach? Your compatriot is a layman and I am merely a little village priest. Surely the proper approach would have been, at the lowest level, through my bishop?'

'One would think so,' I agreed, 'and as we here are in the Anglican diocese of Gibraltar . . . as indeed is the Vatican itself . . . I would say that was the proper channel.'

'In my position, what would you do?'

'While I know little or nothing of ecclesiastical protocol,' I told him, 'why not acquaint your bishop with the facts, leaving him if he thinks fit to communicate with Gibraltar?'

And so we left the matter without any mention being made of Lady Baskerville, the prime mover. Keeping a straight face while with Father Delorme, I chuckled privately over what would happen if he did write to his bishop and if the latter wrote to the Bishop of Gibraltar who might, just might, refer the matter to Canterbury.

From chance remarks here and there I gathered that the projected English church had been received by the British community with something less than enthusiasm. Places like Menton, Nice and Cannes, with far larger British communities, were having a hard time supporting their churches. Another church at Ste Monique would impose an intolerable burden upon the small community. A far more sensible and practical solution of the problem was suggested by several public-spirited Anglicans who offered seats in their cars to those who had no cars, or who would find the journey too tiring. With the opening of the Estérel Autoroute the time of transit had been halved.

The project was allowed to drop, and it is interesting to note that although two British-owned cars made the journey to Cannes every Sunday, or most Sundays, their available seats were not occupied. From this I made the reasonable deduction that the need for an English church was not pressing and that it had existed only in the fevered imagination of Lady Baskerville.

As they say in legal circles, it is not enough that justice be done; it must be seen to be done. So with the doers of Good Works; an essential part of it seems to be that they are seen to be doing Good Works, regardless of whether a need exists. Goldsmith must have had people like that in mind when he eulogized those who do good by stealth and blush to find it fame.

No sooner had the church project been allowed to drop into oblivion than Lady B. turned the spotlight on herself with another Good Work. This time it was a home for stray dogs. I was already familiar with the details when one of Lady B.'s military escort, as I call them, visited me. He was the same tweedy gentleman with a toothbrush moustache concealing a stiff upper lip who had represented himself to Father Delorme as the emissary of the Archbishop of Canterbury.

Somewhat diffidently, I thought, he outlined the project to me. I waited for the commercial before making any observation. 'Is this one of His Grace's projects?' I asked innocently.

'Whose grace?' he barked with a blank look.

'The Archbishop of Canterbury,' I replied. 'I have been given to understand that you represent him here.'

'Who the hell. . . ?' he said, nearly swallowing his bridgework. 'Of course I don't represent him.'

'Then I must have been misinformed,' I said, 'but I assure you that Father Delorme gathered that impression from you.'

Now I am prepared to admit that my visitor was and is a good chap. I know him to be loyal. He served under General Baskerville in India and has since devoted his retirement to the general's widow. Despite being in the sere and yellow leaf in the early eighth decade of his life, trotting about on Lady B.'s errands has given him an air of perennial juvenility. I could go on singing his praises and deservedly, but the fact is that he just isn't my type. I could even produce people who would say that this alone enhances him in their estimation. He is a simple man in the sense of the word that means uncomplicated. It is just that a wet weekend with him would seem too wet.

I gave him a drink to soften the impact of what had to be said. 'I am going to put this to you on patriotic grounds,' I began. 'It has nothing to do with my dislike of Lady B., which I admit freely. We British have a reputation among the French for a certain eccentricity. Whether deserved, or not, isn't important. But to me it is important that it does not go any further. It is an unshakable belief among the French, for example, that we are far more zealous of the comfort and happiness of our animals than we are of people. Have you never noted the splendid housing, good food and care lavished on our thoroughbred horses? Until very recently poor people in England did not fare so well. . . .'

'By Jove! You know, although I never thought of it in that way, you're right.'

'Then I'm sure you'll see my point of view,' I went on. 'I am a dog lover. I abominate any cruelty to dogs, or any animals, even horses. . . .'

'*Even* horses?'

'Yes, it isn't their fault, poor things, that they are out-moded creatures overdue for the evolutionary garbage pit and only permitted to survive for reasons of snobbery and the superstition that sitting on a horse turns a cad into a gentleman. . . .'

'I say, going a bit far, aren't you?'

On sober reflection, it was perhaps going too far, bearing in mind that he had been a Bengal Lancer, or something of the kind.

'Overstating one's case is merely a way of giving emphasis,' I said less militantly.

'Quite, quite.'

'Well, I put it to you as a reasonable man, if we were living in England and a Frenchman arrived on the scene and opened a dogs' home, carrying the clear implication that our dogs needed protection from us, wouldn't you feel annoyed . . . even insulted?'

'Ye-es, I suppose I would.'

'There are two, perhaps more, dogs' homes started by Englishwomen, down on the Riviera proper, to the amused annoyance of the French. . . .'

'Why amused?'

E

'Because elderly Englishwomen with tiny incomes which could not keep pace with the rise in prices have died of starvation ... under a prettier name, of course, and the French know it.'

'That's all very well,' he blustered, 'but two blacks don't make a white and it doesn't help the poor dogs. Do you suggest that we do nothing about it?'

'I suggest,' I told him when he had ceased to quiver with indignation, 'that we leave it to a French person to start this dogs' home and that we, feeling so strongly, contribute to it. Lady Baskerville, of course, will be violently opposed to this because it cheats her of the opportunity of appearing in public as a kind of overweight Joan of Arc. I'll contribute gladly, but I won't aid and abet that stupid old woman in her plan to put an affront on the French when we live in France.'

He didn't like it, but he swallowed hard and took it.

'I'd contribute, too,' he said at length, 'but it wouldn't be much because, like most of us with small fixed incomes, I'm feeling the draught financially. It's all very well for you, of course, but we haven't all got a roulette system that brings the money rolling in whenever you can be bothered going to the casino. Wouldn't like to let me in on it, would you?'

'If I had a system, yes, willingly. But I haven't and I wish I knew who started the story. . . .'

'Lady B. assures me she knows as a fact that you have. . . .'

'She wouldn't know a fact if one dropped on her,' I said tartly.

I was, truth to tell, getting a little tired of being the target for promoters of crank schemes and would-be borrowers, who went away cursing me for my meanness. Denials were sheer waste of time. In some perverse way they seemed to strengthen the belief that I had outsmarted the casinos and had, therefore, a virtually unlimited supply of money on tap. The joke was that over a period of several months I had lost money consistently. Not a great deal of money, but enough to make me cautious and enough to remind me, despite having over the years won far more often

126

than lost, how easy it would be to get into real trouble over gambling.

I not only limit my losses at any one session of play, but I have an overall limit for the winter season which ends in May, after which I stay away from casinos. At this time I was dangerously close to my seasonal limit, so close that I would probably not have played again but for special circumstances.

The grandson of some old friends was getting married. Invited to the wedding and the huge reception afterwards, I felt bound to go. The reception was at Cap Ferrat. I quite enjoyed it and was among the last to leave at around 10 p.m., which is the wrong time to be at a loose end, too early to go home without a sense of let-down. As several other departing guests felt the same way we decided, after a brief discussion, to go to the Riviera Casino to round off the evening.

We reserved a table near the bar, using it as a kind of party headquarters. Some stayed there all the time, while those of us who played did so as lone wolves.

While parking my car I had noticed purely by chance that the mileage read 23032, being the same backwards and forwards. However idiotic it may sound, I decided to bet on 23, zero and 32. It really was not idiotic because these numbers were no more nor less likely to turn up than any others. Choosing numbers in that particular way makes roulette doubly a game of chance.

After about an hour of play with no trend apparent, I began to win. Number 23 turned up twice running and the other two numbers not long afterwards. As I won, so I increased the stakes, ending up a very handsome winner. It was not what could be called a sensational win, but a few people were grouped at the table watching. One of these was another of the retired soldiers who have constituted themselves Lady Baskerville's military escort. He, unknown to me, had also been at the wedding reception. We did not then acknowledge each other, but a little later, when I was turning my chips into cash, I saw him watching me intently with an extremely sour look on his face, which led me to suppose—rightly—that he had been a loser. In my opinion people who look like that when they lose shouldn't play at all, so I turned away. I felt him following me and, sure enough, a few moments later I heard him say: 'You're the chap that has no system, eh? Like hell you haven't!'

He was not drunk, but had drink taken and in just the wrong quantity, enough to make him morose and surly. Having elicited no reply from me, he went on truculently: 'I was talking to you.'

Looking him up and down from his toes to three inches off his left ear, which few people find soothing, I turned on my heel and walked away.

Deciding not to return home that night, I cadged a bed from a friend. In the morning, having paid my loot into the bank, I drove off westwards on the Estérel Autoroute for Ste Monique.

Alphonsine's greeting as I entered the house just before lunch was: 'Now that monsieur has won a great sum at roulette, we can have a new kitchen stove, I hope.'

'Who told you that I had won a great sum?' I asked.

'It is all over the village.'

'Then I shall be obliged to you if you will tell anyone else who says that, that I did not win a great sum. . . .'

'Where did monsieur spend last night?'

'In bed with the chorus of the Folies Bergère, of course, and by the time I had paid them off I did not have enough left for a new kitchen stove.'

With an evil chuckle she went off to prepare lunch.

There followed for me a period of petty annoyance. I probably exaggerate, but it seemed that the only subjects people were willing to discuss with me were the infallible system and my huge—it got bigger with every telling—win at roulette. It amazed me to hear otherwise intelligent people say things which proved that they accepted the idea of the infallible system and were openly envious. I imagine that the winners of football pools must go through the same sort of experience that I did, the target for begging letters, every form of attempted 'touch' ever invented and barbed insults when they failed. I gained some insight into the mentality of the work-shy dropouts who for the most part comprised our artistic colony. They were not only quite shameless in their cadging, but clearly regarded me as their lawful prey.

While my win had not been on anything like the scale suggested to me, I did win, after a long series of losing sessions, a worth-while sum. My intention had been to celebrate the event with some sort of a party, for it had been a longish time since I had done any general entertaining. But the importunities to which I was subjected caused the good intention to wither on the vine, so I contented myself with inviting a few friends to a buffet supper.

If the tumbrils ever roll in Ste Monique, I can count on standing room.

*   *   *   *

I was beginning to wonder when I would hear news from Las Vegas when the post brought me an air mail letter addressed in Esmé's flamboyant style. A large part of the letter has no place here, being a tirade against lawyers and others in the Costa Doradan capital, Santa Eulalia, who were apparently making no headway in the settlement of the family estates. It went on:

Words fail me when it comes to describing this place. Its blatant vulgarity is carried to such a point that it becomes almost magnificent. I was never in a Babylonian brothel, but I think our suite at this fantastic hotel must have been modelled on one. Downstairs the crash, rattle and bang of the slot machines blend into one continuous roar night and day. The gambling is all incredibly noisy. János thinks that the sheer volume of noise dulls the critical faculties and is encouraged for that reason. The gambling may be straight. János is inclined to believe that it is, but who needs to be crooked when the bank has a double zero running for it. Even if one could get near the tables, roulette is not for us here. The entertainments—'floor shows'—are first rate. We go on the nights when János's nose warns against

129

gambling. The food is indescribably awful, all out of freezers and tasting of wet blotting paper. I play nothing but the dice games and, so far, with some success. Dice give one quick action. We go the rounds of a dozen or more places to avoid being too well known at any one. I wear dark glasses sometimes as thousands of other women do. I never dress in quite the same way twice, so I don't think I have attracted any attention. There is a wonderful anonymity here just mingling with the flocks of sheep come to be shorn.

The crooks here look like crooks. If an atom bomb were dropped on Las Vegas it would practically solve the crime problem of the United States. In the next suite to ours is a Sicilian plug-ugly who has been indicted for murder five times and acquitted. The waiter who told us this made it clear that we should feel honoured by being so close to such a celebrity.

There was more, all in a nostalgic vein, suggesting that she wanted to get back to familiar scenes and faces. While I can't quote anything to support it, the letter made me feel uneasy.

14

Not long after this letter from Esmé, I gave a small luncheon party. Among the guests was Pierre Morel, the Grasse perfumer, who stayed behind after the others had gone. 'Do you ever see anything of János Tisza?' he asked when we were alone.

'Not for some months,' I replied. 'He is in the United States.'

'Las Vegas?'

'Whatever made you think that?' I asked, hedging.

'It seemed the most likely place. I've been hearing some most peculiar things about that young man. It is Las Vegas, isn't it?'

I nodded assent. It seemed pointless to deny it.

'Some weird and wonderful stories about him have been going the rounds,' Morel went on. 'Making due allowance for exaggeration, I am inclined to believe that Tisza stumbled on something revolutionary. I remember telling you several years ago that his olfactory sense was outstanding in a place where keen noses have been known for a very long time.

'In our firm's library, which is chiefly concerned with the perfume industry, we have some very old, almost priceless, books and manuscripts. I read some of them for the first time last winter. One of them concerned a Hollander named Van Kuyk, also spelled Van Cuik, who settled in Provence in the sixteenth century and was a familiar of Michel de Notredame, better known to the world as Nostradamus, the astrologer.

'I examined this manuscript most carefully with a view to ascertaining whether it had been opened and read recently. I can state positively that it had not. It would not have surprised me to learn that our young Hungarian friend had read it, for I know that he spent considerable time in the library ... with my permission, I should add. However, the librarian assures me that it was in a locked cupboard which has not been opened for years. It is quite evident, however, that Tisza's mind worked along the same lines as the Hollander's. In brief, Van Kuyk had a phenomenal sense of smell and for a time was employed at a perfumery in the region of Aix-en-Provence where delicately perfumed pomades and various cosmetics were made for the Court.

'Am I boring you?'

'On the contrary,' I replied. 'I find it fascinating.'

'Well, there or elsewhere later, Van Kuyk came to the conclusion that fortune-telling by sense of smell was a possibility, and he set to work to prove it, and it was while engaged in a series of experiments that he met Michel de Notredame, then at the height of his fame. The theory was that just as certain human body odours attract or repel insects or other human beings, so human beings give off odours which attract or repel good and ill fortune. The problem was to identify and classify these odours, a task only within the powers of the kind of man we call a *nez*.

'Now it is being freely said in gambling circles that our friend János Tisza's sensitive nose is well on the way to taming the laws governing what we call chance. If this is only partly true the possibilities are incalculable. As it is also being freely said that you have profited greatly from this discovery, if it is in fact a discovery, I would be most interested to know your views on the subject.'

The cat being now out of the bag, there seemed no point in being discreet. János would never again be allowed to play in any of the Riviera casinos and nothing I could say would do him any harm.

'It is true,' I told Morel, 'that guided by János's predictions I have on several occasions won some money, but it would be true to say that over the many years I have gambled for amusement down here, I have enjoyed some good winning streaks, unaided by anything at all except pure chance. I find myself in the position of a man who goes to two doctors and then has to decide which one cured him. I now confine myself to things I know of my own knowledge, although I am inclined to believe that he has at various times won considerable sums ... he and people playing for him.

'I suppose, in effect, you are asking me to express an opinion about what I call the János system. I think the fairest way to reply is that whereas some while ago I was inclined to ridicule the whole thing, now I regard the probability as being 55:45 that he has something.'

We talked the subject to death, and while I think Morel went away believing that I knew more than I had admitted, which in a sense was true, he asked me to keep in touch and let him know whether there were any fresh developments. 'If he ever comes down here again,' said Morel, 'tell him that all is forgiven and that I bear him no ill will. If he wants to read the Van Kuyk manuscript he is welcome to do so. I say this from pure interest. I am not a gambler and don't want to use his system ... if any.'

In telling Morel what I had, I felt that I had in effect told him nothing, certainly nothing more than he and many others knew, or suspected. Morel evidently regarded the János system as a kind of revival of the Van Kuyk fortune-telling, or prevoyance, not ruling out the possibility of it being pure fakery. I had not disclosed that János claimed to be able to smell imminent good or bad fortune. 'There is nothing general about it,' János had once said to me. 'I am not able to say that this person is generally lucky, or that person generally unlucky. The most I can do is to sense the operation of pure chance in the immediate future. For example, Esmé has on more than one occasion gone on winning when I have sensed that she would win, but if she has gone on playing for more than about an hour, or ninety minutes at most, the luck has changed.'

Casinos are not compelled to give reasons for admitting or excluding people. Nobody has an absolute right of admission. If Chartrain were called upon to justify the exclusion of János and Esmé, I was certain that any reason but the true one would be advanced. It would be enough justification for him to say, without offering evidence in support of it, that they were considered to be undesirable people. When a candidate for membership of a club is blackballed, he has no right to demand disclosure of the reasons. It may not sound fair, but no other procedure is practical. Membership is a privilege, not a right. The risk of being blackballed is one that must be faced, together with the damaging rumours which could follow. Thus, there would always hang an aura of dubiety around János in gambling circles. On the face of things, no casino could afford to say: We have excluded Monsieur X because he wins money too consistently.

The tendency among the uninformed, who are the many, would always be to regard János as a crook and leave it at that.

*　　*　　*　　*

It is easy to be wise after the event, but when the next letter arrived from Esmé, with its horrifying contents, I was not as surprised as I might have been. If the well entrenched gambling interests in Las Vegas were anything remotely near as tough as I believed them to be, they would not take kindly to anyone who, legitimately or not, beat them at their own game. I expected to hear that Esmé and János had been invited to leave, but I was not prepared for the story set down by Esmé. The letter, written from a Los Angeles hospital, read:

Dear Steve: When I tell you how we got here, I doubt whether you will believe me. I'm not quite sure that I believe it myself. Here, briefly, is the story. I will fill in the gaps when we meet which, please God, will be soon.

Well, we made a packet in L.V., but we made the mistake of being too greedy and staying just a little too long. When I tell you that on the day before it all happened we had won $160,000 odd, you will see what I mean. We had already sent bank drafts for most of it to Zurich. With the remainder, $35,000 which we won at the last session, we bought travellers' cheques. I was against playing again, but János insisted that we stay another week. I had an idea we had attracted more notice than was good for us, but J. wouldn't listen.

134

Some Hungarian friends—acquaintances of János—had been engaged for a week as entertainers at one of the big hotels, so we spent an amusing day with them. J. and I returned to our suite around seven o'clock, having arranged to see the others later. When we looked around the suite it was plain that our baggage had been searched. Nothing was as we left it. Nor, as far as we could see, was anything missing. Having lost nothing, it seemed pointless to complain to the management, especially as the management had probably done the searching. By the way it had been done, with little or no effort at concealment, it seemed fairly plain that we were intended to spot it. That seemed to me ominous.

After some little discussion and disagreement, I refused flatly to gamble again and we agreed to dine and take in the cabaret show where J.'s Hungarian friends were, and to leave L.V. in the morning.

Later, when we asked the man on the door to get us a taxi, he produced a handsome limousine. It might cost two or three times a taxi, but what the hell! Instead of taking us to our destination, the driver took one of the roads out into the desert. J. banged on the glass partition but the man took no notice. By now I was so scared I was wetting myself. I expect J. was too. The car pulled off the road a short way alongside a ramshackle old car that looked more like an abandoned wreck. Our driver opened the door and ordered us to get out. Two men came out of the darkness. They went through my handbag and J.'s pockets, taking all the money they found and the travellers' cheques. We were hustled into the old ruin of a car. The two men sat in the front seats and we moved off at a slow speed without lights. After some twenty minutes the car stopped. We were hauled out. The only words spoken from start to finish were: 'Git goin' and don't come back.' The car drove off and left us.

I was wearing satin slippers. J. was wearing a thin suit and lightweight suède shoes. My fur jacket and his overcoat had been left in the first car and, you may believe me, it was bloody cold.

We followed the car's tyre tracks, hoping to get back to the highway, but these petered out in a few hundred yards. Neither of us knew how to navigate by the stars, so all we could do was to guess the direction. When I say desert I mean desert, a howling wilderness of nothing, blazing hot in the day and brutally cold at night. We had to walk to maintain circulation. We walked for four hours. Then my slippers gave up the ghost. J.'s shoes were badly cut and not much better. To avoid getting cut feet we stopped until daylight.

At eight in the morning it was pleasantly warm. At nine it was too warm and after that it was so bloody hot that I couldn't think. We unpicked the back seam of J.'s jacket, using half each as protection for our heads. We walked for an hour or more until we found what I think must have been an old mine shaft. On one side was a heap of waste which gave us some shade. We moved round with the sun. J. was in a bad way by afternoon. He was less accustomed to heat than I was.

The sun was low in the West when we ran across tyre tracks. They ran two ways. One would have taken us to the highway, the other away from it. We tossed a coin and just as the light began to fade we heard the noise of cars running at speed. They were using headlights when we reached the road. We stood on the verge of the road trying to make one stop, but would you believe it, the buggers seemed to go faster. We were just about all in. I was beginning to see things. Then J. had the bright idea which saved our bacon. A few hundred yards from us, picked up by car headlights, was the wreck of a car. I wouldn't be surprised if it had happened that day. Anyway, J. unscrewed the cap on the petrol tank, soaked a newspaper we found in the car and put a match to it. He was lucky he only lost his hair. The car went off in a sheet of flame that must have been visible for miles. Assuming that we had just crawled out of the wreck, a car stopped. A couple called Hartland, or Hartman—I'd like to thank them if I knew where to find them—gave us whisky and ice water and were kind enough not to bother us with stupid questions. I remember nothing more of the drive. I was out like a light and the next thing I remember was lying in bed at this hospital. I heard someone say, 'Shock, sunburn and exposure.' Then someone said, 'Her feet are like raw beef.'

We had no money, but I have a cousin who lives in L.A. The hospital people got him on the phone and he did what was necessary. They tell me I shall have to stay where I am for a few more days. J. more than that. A warning has

136

been sent out that our travellers' cheques are stolen. We shall get a refund when they get around to it.

I asked my cousin to make some sort of a formal complaint to the Nevada police. His reply was: 'Don't waste your time. You won a lot of money, didn't you? That makes you the criminals in that state.'

Love,
Esmé

Having read the letter twice, I find comment superfluous. Perhaps the most alarming thing about it was that the gangsters who control Las Vegas gambling through their dummies are the same people alleged to have moved in on British organized gambling. If true—and my knowledge is confined to what I read—it is a bad day for us.

Esmé's next letter followed ten days later. In it she said that when they had bought some things for the journey— none of their belongings were recovered from the hotel— they would be coming to Europe.

I next heard from them at a sort of nursing and convalescent home in Sussex. I was visiting London when I heard this and drove down to see them. There was nothing physically wrong with them then, I was told, but they needed complete rest and no excitement. Both had suffered severe shock. Esmé could not talk about it without getting excited, so I did not stay long. János did not seem at all excited, but I knew how hard it was to read what was going on behind that inscrutable Hungarian face. When I left, he was asleep in front of a television set, while she was reading Jane Austen. The experience, I decided, *must* have been a shock. Jane Austen would be good for her.

Esmé and her father confirmed my belief that, just as there are accident-prone people, so there are disaster-prone. These last go at life full tilt and life repays them in kind. It is a waste of time warning them of dire happenings for, even if successful, one is made to feel thereafter that one has cheated them of some vital experience. It is vain to hope that they will learn prudence: they never do. Fulfilment of their destiny is to be overwhelmed. But, on the opposite side of the ledger, they have a lot of fun which the rest of us miss.

On my return home to Ste Monique, among the letters awaiting me was one from a firm of solicitors unknown to me. I cannot quote it in detail as I sent it on to János. The gist of it was that their client, who was not named, urgently desired to be put in touch with Mr János Tisza. Their letter was addressed to me in the hope that I would know his whereabouts.

I wrote to them saying that I had passed over their letter to János from whom, if he were interested, they would doubtless hear. From enquiries I made later, it emerged by chance that this firm, whose reputation was quite good, had a theatrical and sporting clientèle. My guess, which happened to be right, was that 'sporting' was another name for 'gambling'.

The Esmé who arrived in Ste Monique about three weeks after I did wore a chastened air, as well she might. She never went out unless with me. She joined me at meals, spent most of her time reading and went to bed early. Alphonsine clucked over her like a broody hen.

We did not talk about Las Vegas, or its unpleasant aftermath. I don't think gambling was ever mentioned between us. I left it for her to broach the subject if she wanted to. She had been with me for a couple of weeks before she did so.

'It has only just occurred to me,' she said thoughtfully, 'but János and I won what I call the wrong amount of money, a pleasant sum to win if you like, but not enough to really solve any problems permanently.'

'In point of fact,' I asked, 'what did you win all told?'

'After paying all expenses, which weren't peanuts, János and I took about £52,000 each, or its equivalent. That should yield seven per cent in safety before tax. If I live anywhere where there is income-tax the £3,500 would be reduced to not much more than £2,000. That's a mechanic's wage today. In case you don't know it, Steve, I've got expensive tastes.'

'Then live somewhere where you won't have to pay

income-tax, or somewhere where it won't be a great burden. . . .'

'Such as?'

'Switzerland.'

'God forbid! I'd die of boredom.'

'Then Spain.'

'Spain's even worse. It would be a race between being bored to death or starved to death. No, Spain's just a little too Spanish for me.'

'Then what?' I asked. 'I hope you're not thinking of going in with János again?'

'I don't see what else I can do,' she said.

'Marry.'

'Yes, naturally, I've thought about marriage, but I don't have to tell you of all people that I'm . . . well, a trifle shop-soiled. I'd feel obliged to tell my future husband all about my little fornications and he might not like it. Some men are funny that way. Mark you, Steve, I don't want to go back to that bloody haunting of gambling hells. If I could choose, I'd never put a foot inside one again. If I could choose. . . .'

'I wish now,' I told her, 'that I had never introduced you and János. I would have spared you a lot of trouble. Not that I blame János for anything. He is as he is made and I should have recognized it. Nobody is really at fault. In these matters "fault" is the wrong word. Only a chemist understands that some chemicals when united make a smell, while if the proportions are changed you get an explosion. . . .'

'In the meantime,' said Esmé, with a grin, 'my problem is to lay my hands on some more money. Maybe there'll be a bad smell, or an explosion. If so, *tant pis.*'

The best hope now was that János would not come back into Esmé's life, but I knew the hope was a vain one.

139

15

János had been back in Ste Monique for more than two weeks, staying with his Belgian friends, before I saw him, and when I did at last see him I was shocked by his appearance. He came to lunch and, as I had been warned that he would not speak of his experiences at Las Vegas, we talked of almost everything else imaginable. But it was a strain and I was glad when Esmé drove him home.

'There's nothing wrong with him physically,' Esmé told me. 'The doctors told us that when we were staying at the convalescent home in Sussex.'

'Do you mean that it's something mental?' I asked.

'Not if you take that to mean that he's gone round the bend,' she replied. 'But there *is* something spiritually wrong, something deep down inside him. He is consuming himself with rage and frustration because of that awful time in the desert. He blames himself for being such a simpleton. If you knew János as well as I think I'm beginning to, you would know that he has a need, in order to be able to live with himself, for being smarter than anyone else. So he is . . . most of the time. But at Las Vegas he was not. So all his rage, hatred and resentment are concentrated on Las Vegas and, in particular, a smooth article we knew slightly as "Mister Bell" whose real name is Belloni, an ex-gangster prettied up, wearing a big grin and very sincere clothes.

'János, by making enquiries, has learned that this Belloni is the chief shareholder in the gilded honky-tonk where we stayed and has shares in other gambling hells. In other words, he's a big noise out there. János seems to know a lot about him. How I don't pretend to know. If János heard now that this Belloni had been run over by a bus, he'd be back to his old form by tomorrow morning. I'd feel inclined to give three hearty British cheers, too . . . the bastard.'

'If János is right. . . .' I said.

'János nearly always is right.'

Although Esmé had, in her usual fashion, overstated the case, I felt she was somewhere near the mark, anyway about János himself. But I did not rule out the possibility that exposure to the blazing desert sun might be responsible in part for his condition. He and Esmé had been extremely lucky to survive. I have driven a car from Las Vegas to Hollywood in May, well before the great heat, but even then it was frighteningly hot.

Privately, because I liked János, I hoped that the experience had given him a big scare and that he would settle down to some more normal livelihood.

All I know about Las Vegas is not much. I spent a night there on the way across the country, but I did not gamble and I saw the blaze of neon from a distance only. It was close enough. Friends who do know the place give it a truly evil reputation.

*   *   *   *

One day I ran into Chartrain by accident on the island of Porquerolles, where we were both lunching with different parties. 'I would very much like a chat with you,' he said. 'It isn't practical here, so may I telephone you?'

At my suggestion he agreed to come to lunch a few days thence. I chose a day when Esmé would, I knew, be elsewhere. Whatever it was that Chartrain wanted to see me about, it just had to be about János, Esmé or both.

On the day fixed he wasted no time coming to the point. We were drinking an apéritif in the garden. 'I feel that in excluding our young Hungarian friend from the casino we were somewhat hasty,' he began. 'If he would like to have his card of admission restored, I feel sure that it can be arranged, and if I can call upon your good offices to arrange a meeting, I would be most grateful.'

'He is, as you may know, an ill man,' I told him, 'and I

141

have only seen him once since I returned. I will, of course, tell him what you say. But I am inclined to doubt whether he would accept another card. He was, I do not mind telling you, mortally affronted when his card was withdrawn . . . and that of Madame Latta.'

Chartrain received this in silence. He was, I felt, more put out than the circumstances warranted. It could be of no great importance whether János was received back into the fold or not.

'Forgive me asking,' I said, before the subject was dropped, 'but would your interest be connected with the so-called "infallible system" I have heard about from several quarters?'

'It is, to be frank with you, not entirely unconnected,' he replied, causing me to guffaw impolitely.

He laughed, too, and all was well.

Chartrain could not possibly be concerned about any repercussions in connection with the withdrawal of the cards, because the casino had, unquestionably, been within their rights. That left only the system. It would emerge.

'What do you think is behind his interest?' János asked when I told him of the conversation.

'They just might believe you have a system and want to buy it off you,' I said.

'Leaving me free to play the system again, or sell it to someone else?'

That made sense.

'When I am feeling better,' he said, after a thoughtful pause, 'I will see the man. There is nothing to lose and, perhaps, something to gain. Why not?'

My intention at that time was to drop out of the picture altogether, leaving János and Chartrain to extract what nourishment they could from each other without my help. It was not that I was not curious to learn what eventuated. On the contrary, understanding something of what actuated both of them, my curiosity to learn the outcome was boundless. My attitude otherwise was simply that, liking both men and having no personal axe to grind, I did not want to

142

become too deeply involved. My intention to hold aloof came to nothing because, once a meeting had been arranged, each of the two without the other's knowledge asked me to be present. The upshot was that, with Chartrain as host, we dined at a fish place on the ramparts of Antibes. The meal passed pleasantly enough, each of the two protagonists weighing up the other. Chartrain, being the older and more experienced man, seemed to me to have the advantage, but then I had not seen János as a negotiator.

'Now, Monsieur Tisza,' said Chartrain when the coffee and liqueurs had been brought, 'perhaps we may discuss this clever system you have invented. . . .'

'What system?' asked János, looking astonished. 'I do not claim to have invented any system. If we have met to discuss one, then I fear I have enjoyed your delightful hospitality under false pretences.'

In turn they looked at me, but all they got out of me was a shrug of the shoulders.

'Perhaps,' said Chartrain at length, 'system is the wrong word. Would "method of play" be more correct?'

'Yes, that fits the case perfectly,' said János suavely. 'After all, everyone has his method of play.'

'And yours, I am sure you will admit,' said the other, 'has been remarkably successful . . . here and elsewhere.'

'It has had its ups and downs, but on the whole it has been most satisfactory.'

They sparred in this way for several minutes, getting precisely nowhere.

'Permit me to be quite blunt, Monsieur Tisza, as our Anglo-Saxon friends'—he smiled at me—'sometimes are. I applaud it for it clears the air. Now it is plain to me, Monsieur Tisza, and to many others whose business is to observe and report, that whether you have a system, which you do not specifically deny, or a method of play, the pattern of your gains has been too consistent to be, shall we say, normal. . . .'

'Because the normal player loses, does he not, Monsieur Chartrain? That, surely, is how casinos exist?'

'Of course, and you may believe me that we have a vast

fund of experience to draw upon. I have known pure chance to enable a player to win ten times as much as you have won ... from the Riviera Casino, that is, and I could cite examples from among thousands which, if I did not know them to be completely factual, I would find quite incredible. Chance works in such strange patterns that one is sometimes tempted to believe that it is governed by some mischievous child with a perverted sense of humour. But this mischievous child, if you will permit me the continued use of the analogy, Monsieur Tisza, has not the staying power to maintain the pattern of gains over such an extended period as you have enjoyed them. If pure chance is the only factor involved—and please read nothing pejorative into this— such things just do not happen. . . .'

'And you do not admit the possibility of a first time?' asked János, cocking an eyebrow.

'No, Monsieur Tisza, I do not, and again, let me say, there is no dishonourable action imputed to you. I go further. If I could evolve, invent, discover a system, or method of play, as successful as yours has been, I would resign from my post and go on a world tour in the height of luxury to exploit it for the rest of my days. You do not cheat. You have been too carefully observed for that to be possible. You do not suborn casino employees. So what else is left ... except pure chance, which good sense and long experience do not permit me to accept.'

János gave a slight bow. 'Then it does not seem clear to me, Monsieur Chartrain, how can I serve you. Matching your admirable bluntness ... what do you want of me?'

'Very well, I will tell you. I want to know just precisely how you have achieved this long succession of gains, here and elsewhere.'

This harping on 'here and elsewhere' was, presumably, for the purpose of telling János that his activities in London and, perhaps, on the other side of the Atlantic, were known to him.

János had a charmingly innocent smile, seldom used and the more effective for that. He switched it on. 'If I tell you, Monsieur Chartrain and, of course, if there is anything to tell, what is there in it for me? I imagine that you do not expect me to disclose this infallible system merely because I have a kind heart. Now that our cards—anyway, some of our cards—are on the table, I will admit that I anticipated this moment in our relations and, let me say, with some perplexity.

'Supposing that you are a buyer, I ask myself what I have to sell. Putting myself in your position, I ask myself how, if I sell, you can be sure that I stay bought. . . .'

'Then you admit that you have something to sell?'

'I admit nothing, Monsieur Chartrain. You yourself cannot have failed to ask these questions and to have reached the same conclusions as I have. Now I am perplexed to know where it has led you. Where do we go from here?'

'Your system. . . .'

'One moment, please, Monsieur Chartrain. I do not resent your use of the word "system" but I must point out to you that you have no evidence that I employ a system or, if you have, you have not adduced it. I certainly make no such claim. You and that young man with the curiously shaped head, who has an eagle's eye for systems, have failed to establish that I have one. Is that not so? You have on paper, for perusal at your leisure, a record of every stake made by me or made by anyone playing for me, over a long period of months, down to the last detail. Be frank and admit that from the study of it no pattern of any kind emerged . . . except the paradoxical one that there was no pattern.'

'That is obvious, Monsieur Tisza, for if a pattern had emerged we should not be sitting here having this delightful conversation.'

'But surely,' said János, pressing home his advantage, 'you must admit that nobody living could play by a system for months, under the keen eyes of experts, without that system becoming apparent? Systems leave plainer trails than cryptograms and these, sooner or later, are always solved.'

'I am inclined to agree with you,' said the other with

145

pursed lips, 'so let the word "system" not be heard again between us. Let me tell you instead of something said by the young man with a peculiarly shaped head. He was speaking of the so charming Madame Latta. "She plays like one inspired," he said of one particular evening. 'Roulette as she plays it is not a game of chance. She places her stake, turns away from the table as though she has lost interest and shows no surprise when the little ivory ball goes where directed. There has never been the smallest sign of strain or anxiety observable in her. If she had been born a few centuries earlier, she would have been burned as a witch." Let me add that the young man who said that to me is not at all fanciful. Very much the contrary.'

'In view of what you say,' said János blandly, 'what can I possibly have to sell you? Supernatural powers, as I am sure the best sorcerers would agree, cannot be bought and sold like beans.'

The silence which fell on the little party was more eloquent than words, for it seemed to say that everything which could be said had been said. 'Allow me to thank you for a most delightful evening,' said János, breaking it. 'I am glad also that any misunderstanding has been ended.'

Another silence.

'I hope you will forgive me, János,' I said at length, 'but are you not being a little obtuse? Monsieur Chartrain wants something. That is why he is here. You know what that something is. He does not. How, therefore, can he be expected to put it into concise words? By a method which you alone know you have won more money than, shall we say, is consistent with a game in which chance is the only factor, even after you have overcome the percentage of odds in favour of the casino. Let us call your method X. Monsieur Chartrain has invited you to put a price on X. If you are ready to sell, barter, lend or otherwise dispose of it, now is your chance to name your price.'

'If skills could be bought and transformed to the buyer,' János replied thoughtfully, 'a rich man, if he so desired, could become a world champion chess player, footballer or

146

skater. But, as we three know, that is an absurdity. My method of play, which we call X, is in precisely that category. It is mine, inseparably mine. I could explain it to you, but it would be implicit in our bargain that you could harness X to your own uses. But I assure you, Monsieur Chartrain, that you could not. I am, whether you believe it or not, a reasonably honest man, and I will not accept money from you only to have you afterwards say that I cheated you by selling you something I could not deliver. Believe me, I understand and sympathize with your predicament, and I must ask you to understand mine.'

'Then it seems we have reached an impasse,' said Chartrain almost sadly, 'unless you have any suggestion to make.'

'As evidence of my good will,' said János at length, 'I will make one suggestion. It is that, having restored our admission cards to Madame Latta and myself, you allow her, me, or us to play any game of our choice under the normal rules of the casino governing that game, with the same minimum and maximum limits. We will submit, if you wish, to bodily search so that you can satisfy yourself that no apparatus is being introduced. You may surround her, me or us with your system detector and other experts, and you may take any precautions you please against trickery, always provided that there is no public humiliation involved to either of us. If under these conditions I lose money, it is yours. If I win money, it is mine . . . with the proviso that if any trickery is proved against me—and by trickery I mean anything dishonest—I forfeit all my winnings over the period agreed . . . one to three months should suffice. I am further prepared, by mutual agreement, to have my winnings held in escrow against such an eventuality. Does that strike you as fair?'

'Would you agree to the sum of your winnings being limited?' asked Chartrain.

'No, nor would I ask for my losses to be limited.'

Chartrain was interested. 'In a matter such as this, Monsieur Tisza, I would have to consult my co-directors. I think I can promise you a reply to your proposal in ... say, three days.'

On that note the party broke up.

'If he agrees,' said János as we went to the car, 'I shall win far more than he would ever agree to pay for my method, and at the end the poor man will be as wise as he is now.'

Within the three days there was a phone call from Chartrain saying that, subject to one or two minor changes in the proposal, the directors had agreed. One of the changes was not quite so minor. Would János pledge himself on his honour to reveal his method if it were not discovered before the end of the experiment. János, to my astonishment, agreed and he insisted that all play should be public, but that the public should not be made aware of what was afoot.

Chartrain agreed to this, suggesting to me that János had managed to give them a fright. I could understand that. From the day when a man first hid his small treasures in a hollow tree, a ding-dong warfare has been waged between the owner of property and the thief. It still goes on between the safe-maker and the safe-breaker, each side aware that advantage is only temporary. So with casinos and individual gamblers. Casinos have been and will again be outsmarted by the clever or the crooked and casino managements know that to survive they must keep abreast of any new method of looting their coffers. Chartrain and his colleagues did not really believe that János was a threat to their existence, but they dared not take the chance that he might be, and in order to buy peace of mind they were willing to lose some money. That, at least, was how I summarized the position.

At János's insistence a memorandum of agreement was drawn up in writing and initialled by both parties, to be given to whoever agreed to be the stakeholder of János's winnings, who would act as a kind of referee. I doubt if any of it would have held water in law, but it made János happy and did no harm. I did not believe that Chartrain and his colleagues would act in bad faith, for a casino's reputation for scrupulously fair dealing is probably its most valuable asset.

'At the end of the experiment,' I asked János, 'will you tell them how you do it?'

'Yes, why not? I can afford to be honest. They will probably not believe me, but I cannot help that. If they believe me, then every *nez* in Grasse and elsewhere will be watched every time they come into the casino. Also some of the wine tasters, tea tasters too, perhaps, and any others known to have a highly developed sense of smell or taste.'

'And what about you? They will most certainly bar you for life, as will every casino in Europe.'

'I am already barred. What do I care? By then I shall have made enough money to keep me for the rest of my life. . . .'

'You hope.'

'Yes, I hope. I hope then I shall be finished with gambling. It is very boring and I am tired of it.'

A few days after this I saw János in the *place* at Ste Monique, walking with a small, dapper man wearing patent leather shoes which went to a fine point and a blue silk suit of exaggerated modern cut. His hair, being a colour that nature would not recognize, was plainly dyed, unless he wore a wig. He was over-barbered and, despite a brilliant smile, looked dangerous. A thoroughly nasty piece of work, in short, was my summation.

My friend Lentrua's judgment coincided with mine. He and I were chatting over coffee when János entered the bar with the man in question. 'If that one offered to sell me louis d'or at ten centimes apiece, I would not buy them. A hard one!' When János made as though to join us, I shook my head and turned my back somewhat ostentatiously. Sometimes one must meet unpleasant people, but to do so without need is, as I see it, wanton.

I am constantly hearing that one should not judge by appearances, to which I feel inclined to reply that one should not judge at all. In a perfect world that would be so. I judge a wasp by its appearance, so why not something potentially far more deadly ... a man? This man had reptilian eyes. His sinuous movements, accentuated by the sleekness of his clothes, suggested a snake. I don't like snakes. What is so uncharitable about that? As well to say that it is uncharitable to come in out of the rain.

When I next saw János, he told me that the man was a Sicilian-American with the good old Irish name of McGuire. He represented London gambling interests. He had hinted at much, but said little. If János would go to London, all expenses paid of course, it might turn out very much to his advantage. I wouldn't cross a country lane on that inducement.

'It looks as though the boys are rattled,' I said. 'Your best bet is to hold an auction.'

As soon as I had said that I knew how foolish it was. The people who run gambling hells ... clubs if you find the other too old-fashioned ... are not gamblers. Gambling is for their dupes. They are sure thing artists who never take a chance on anything unless on their pasts catching up with them. 'On second thoughts,' I corrected myself, 'your best bet is to have nothing whatever to do with the chap.'

'I won't,' said János, 'unless I can think of a way of being smarter than he is.'

That flat Hungarian nose had already led him down some strange ways, which were getting stranger. His real trouble was one of imbalance of the senses. He lived through his nose. For the rest, he was tone deaf. The beauty he 'saw' in nature was the scent of flowers. A sense of touch was lacking. Delicate textures meant nothing to him. The fabric of the clothes he wore was so coarse to the touch that it would have set my teeth on edge, but I am convinced that he was not aware of it. Yet I remember a day early in our acquaintance when, apparently apropos of nothing, he said, crinkling his nose : 'You've worn that suit in London.'

'How did you know that?' I asked, for it was so.

'Because it smells of London,' he replied, looking astonished that I could ask such a question.

In a room full of people all strange to him, he could pair

off those who lived together. Each one of us, he said, had a distinctive smell. Each of two people who lived together retained his own distinctive odour, but with an overtone of the other person, instantly recognizable.

On the whole, I would prefer more balanced senses. With my own not very keen sense of smell, I suffer enough on a bus in hot weather.

*　　*　　*　　*

There was quite a reception committee to greet János and Esmé in Chartrain's private office at the Riviera Casino. This was the first evening of the experimental three months during which János, under the eyes of the best brains the casino could muster, was going to demonstrate his 'method of play'. At his insistence the word 'system' was not used. I had been invited, too.

Early in the proceedings János threw a spanner into the works by announcing: 'I regret that it is not possible for us to play this evening.'

'But why?' asked Chartrain in dismay.

'We cannot win every evening,' replied János, 'and this is one of the evenings when we would lose.'

'How can you possibly know such a thing?'

'This is not Madame Latta's evening. But if you doubt me, by all means let us watch her play ... with your money, of course. Her winnings, if any, would be yours.'

With a puzzled expression on his face, Chartrain gave Esmé 500 francs in chips and invited her to play for him. Esmé led the way into the *salle des jeux* and the rest of us followed at discreet intervals so as to avoid attracting attention. Esmé went immediately to the *trente et quarante* table. I went to a place at the table diagonally opposite to hers. *Trente et quarante* offers only even money chances. Esmé began with twenty-five twenty-franc chips. I changed my 500 francs into ten fifty-franc chips. In fifteen to twenty minutes from starting to play Esmé was down to her last piece, which she then lost. From start to finish I bet against her, fifty to her twenty, so that I won just two and a half times what she lost. In point of fact it did not work out as exactly that, but nearly enough.

Chartrain, who had been watching me as well as Esmé, looked impressed.

'For the future, Monsieur Chartrain,' said János, 'I suggest for your convenience that I notify you by telephone whether, or not, on the evening in question, we shall be playing. We must not be so foolish as to play when the fairies tell us not to.'

'Please satisfy my curiosity on one point, Monsieur Tisza,' Chartrain said. 'Why did you not do as Monsieur Lister did, play against Madame Latta?'

'I once thought that would be possible,' János replied, 'but in practice it is not. Madame Latta and I are partners. Her luck is, therefore, my luck. I cannot play against myself.'

I could not find fault with it. Nor could the others.

'It worked with Monsieur Lister. . . .'

'Who is not a partner. He has no financial interest whatsoever in our play.'

'But surely, Monsieur Tisza,' said the man with the curiously shaped head, 'forgetting Madame Latta . . . if it were possible to forget such a charming lady . . . surely you have luck of your own?'

'Doubtless I have, monsieur, but the only way I can ascertain whether it is good or bad is to play. Then it is too late.'

'*Sans indiscretion,* Monsieur Tisza,' said the same man, 'may I ask when and where you were born?'

'I was born on the shores of Lake Balaton, in Hungary, on 16 June 1929.'

'At what time of day, if I may enquire?'

'I cannot be more precise than to say it was during the hours of darkness, between midnight and dawn. Once when I was about twenty years of age my horoscope was cast by an eminent astrologer, who warned me that I must never gamble.'

'Then it would seem that you did not take his warning very seriously,' remarked Chartrain with a smile.

'On the contrary,' said János. 'I have that warning constantly in my mind. *I do not gamble.*'

He did not add that he only bet on certainties, but that was the sense and emphasis of his words, said with such quiet assurance that it impressed those who heard it, bringing the talk to a stop. Anything more would have been anti-climactic.

Chartrain was just one more example of the truth that we believe what we want to believe. Despite being a shrewd, hard-headed man of the world, and he was all that, he still found room for that streak of gullibility which is found in the least expected people. The next time I saw him he buttonholed me at the bar of the casino, our usual meeting place.

'The whole thing is easy to understand now,' he said. 'I don't know why it was not apparent long ago. . . .'

I waited.

'Do you think,' he went on in conspiratorial fashion, 'that you could possibly ascertain Madame Latta's birth date and, if possible, the hour.'

'Nothing would be easier,' I replied. 'I will ask her. But why do you want to know?'

'That question is not worthy of you,' he said pityingly. 'I have never given much thought to astrology, but it is quite plain to me now that either Monsieur Tisza is himself an eminent astrologer, or he has one working for him in the background. You noted, I expect, that Monsieur Tisza does not know the hour of his birth. He said, therefore, that he has no way of ascertaining his own luck until he plays. As the leading astrologers will tell you, hours, indeed often minutes, are of vital importance in their calculations. Something else now comes back to me. In the days when Monsieur Tisza was often to be seen here I noticed, and so did others, that he consulted his watch as many as a dozen times an hour. Time, therefore, was . . . and is an important factor in his system . . . I withdraw that word . . . in his method of play. Can you tell me of any other conceivable manner in which chance and time are so inextricably linked? Do you begin to see it now?'

'Now that you have explained it to me so succinctly, I do

begin to see,' I said, having difficulty in keeping my face straight. 'I imagine now that you will waste no time closing this establishment forever. It is very sad. I shall miss it, for I have spent so many pleasant hours here.'

'Monsieur amuses himself at my expense,' said Chartrain, going all po-faced.

'Not at all,' I said. 'If Monsieur Tisza—let us for the future call him the Hungarian Astrologer—can peer thus clearly into the future, there must be many others. The bookshops are full of books about astrology. In the Nice-Matin every day there are the announcements of astrologers from whom, they claim, nothing is hidden. It is a bad outlook for you. Indeed, my heart goes out to you in this tragic hour.'

The corners of his mouth turned down. 'There is a time and place for everything, monsieur,' he said primly.

'Forgive me, Monsieur Chartrain,' I said contritely. 'In this Temple of Mammon I should have been more respectful.'

16

It was by pure chance that I happened to be in the casino during the evening of the day on which János, in accordance with the understanding reached, had notified Chartrain of his intention to play after an interval of more than a week. I found him rubbing his hands with glee. I had, with Esmé's permission, let him have the details of her birth ... place, date and approximate time. This in turn he had passed over to one of the leading astrologers on the coast, requesting him to concentrate on favourable, or unfavourable, signs for a gambler. 'This evening, if my astrologer is to be believed,' Chartrain told me, 'Madame Latta is certain to lose. She could not have chosen a worse evening to play.'

'Remember, Monsieur Chartrain,' I said warningly, 'that Madame Latta is an old friend and a guest in my house. I might be tempted to tell her of your astrologer's warning.'

'Tell her, my friend, by all means tell her. It will be interesting to see her reaction.'

'I doubt whether her reaction is of much importance,' I said. 'That of our friend the Hungarian Astrologer may well be. It is he who directs the whole operation.'

At that moment Esmé and János arrived, and in Chartrain's presence I passed on the astrologer's warning.

'I would be most interested to know the nationality of the astrologer,' said János with polite interest.

'He is a Czech,' said Chartrain, after a brief hesitation. 'Does that make any difference?'

'Does it make any difference?' János echoed in mock horror. 'Let me assure you, Monsieur Chartrain, that in Hungary we have known for centuries that no Czech ever speaks the truth.'

'It is evident by your presence here this evening, Monsieur

155

Tisza,' said the other with a perplexed air, 'that you read a different story from the stars and that they are the same stars.'

János neither admitted nor denied anything. Instead he smiled a serene, Buddha-like smile which might have meant anything and in fact meant nothing. At no time had János made any claim to being an astrologer. It had been done for him. Thus and from such flimsy material are reputations made.

Esmé elected to play roulette that evening, and in some twenty odd minutes of insane, reckless and altogether unsystematic play shattered forever the reputation of the Czech astrologer. Just how much she won I do not know, but it was enough to make the usually impassive croupier exchange a look of dismay with Chartrain.

'I hope, Monsieur Chartrain,' said János afterwards, 'that you did not pay that Czech anything.' The other was not amused.

On the strength of his winnings János invited me to dine at one of the most expensive sucker traps on the coast, where to call the food mediocre was fulsome flattery. I made the counter-suggestion that we go to a place vastly superior at about a quarter the probable price. It then transpired that János had already invited a young compatriot to meet him at the first place. 'His name is Kun,' he explained. 'He is a nice chap, but a bloody fool. He gambles,' János added, as though that accounted for everything.

Bearing in mind the circumstances of the evening, this struck me as being highly amusing. Reading my thoughts correctly, János added: 'Gambling is for fools. I do not gamble.'

Having a little time to kill, Esmé, János and I went to the near-by Baccara Bar, where it quickly became apparent that all was not sweetness and light between the other two. What it was all about I did not know, or want to know. They bickered. They may even have enjoyed it, but I did not. 'If you two can't open your mouths without snarling at each other,' I said at length, 'you can include me out.'

When I rose to leave, Esmé anticipated me. 'I have my

car near here,' she said, 'so I'll go home alone.' With that she disappeared.

Kun was waiting for us at the table which had been reserved by phone. He had ordered and nearly finished a bottle of vintage Krug, either because he knew champagne, or because it was the most expensive one on the wine card.

Despite the poor food and Esmé's defection, it turned out to be a most amusing evening. Kun was largely responsible. Half of the stories he told us were lies. Of that I felt sure. But which half was true and which untrue I could not even guess.

He and János had known each other as boys when they both lived in a town with an unpronounceable name a few miles from Budapest. Kun, if he were to be believed, was an unfrocked priest. There had been some little trouble concerning a beautiful soprano, member of a choral society in whose affairs Kun, as a priest, played an important part. The Church at the time had been under communist fire and it had seemed expedient to the bishop of the diocese to make an example of the offender. 'There is a moral to the story,' he said deadpan, 'for it illustrates the power of a beautiful woman for good or evil. In this case, of course, it was for good.'

I must have looked as surprised as I felt, for he went on: 'Surely you cannot doubt that the lady rendered the Church a great service by helping it to get rid of a bad priest?'

All this was in a mixture of grammatically correct French and English, both so heavily accented as to be irresistibly comic.

It emerged as the evening wore on that Kun was in an unenviable predicament. He had lost all his available cash at the casino, added to which he was being pressed for payment of his hotel bill. While I cannot believe that he was other than worried, he gave no least sign of it, appearing quite unconcerned. To me he was just another Hungarian who enjoyed living dangerously.

Summer had come again and, as I never set foot in a casino between May and October, I lost touch with events

157

in so far as they concerned János and his efforts to 'beat the bank', except on his increasingly rare visits to Ste Monique. Although, despite his hot denials that he was a gambler, he was, like every gambler I ever met, fathoms deep in superstition. He believed that it brought ill-luck to talk about winnings, so I did not learn from him how the campaign progressed. He seemed disgruntled. Esmé was the cause of it, having on several occasions failed to turn up at the casino after János had advised Chartrain that he would play. I did not mention to him that I also was somewhat disgruntled although for different reasons.

Esmé was still occupying the guest cottage, but so far as any companionship was concerned, she might have been staying anywhere. I like a little companionship from my guests, which is why I had the cottage built in the first instance. When she did turn up for meals, she was moody and silent. After dinner she frequently sat for hours pretending to read a book and ignoring my existence. What she was really doing was waiting for the phone to ring, and when it did not she went off to bed in high dudgeon.

'I saw János yesterday,' I told her on one occasion, 'and he seemed to think you were not treating him fairly ... breaking appointments and so on.'

'Let him think what he bloo- ... what he likes,' she amended.

'If you're not going to keep up your end of the partnership,' I told her, 'surely the least you can do is to tell him so?'

'Suppose you mind your own goddamn business and I'll mind mine. I'm sorry, Steve, I shouldn't have said that. Things are turning me into a sour-tempered bitch.'

'As long as I've known you, you've always been that. What's the particular trouble now? If I can help, let me.'

'Thanks all the same, Steve, but nobody can help me. I got into this by myself and I'll have to get out of it the same way. János has been very fair and generous, but I'm sick to death of the whole sordid business. I never want to see a casino again . . . all those ghastly people with spidery predatory hands, empty eyes, looking like damned souls at the gates of hell. . . .'

'If you feel like that,' I said, 'pack it up, quit, forget it, but at least have the decency to tell János your intentions.'

'But it isn't as simple as that,' she protested. 'I need the money and I don't know any other way of getting it. What makes it all so much worse is that I know gambling is basically dishonest.'

'No,' I interrupted, 'there's nothing dishonest about gambling . . . anyway about honest gambling. It's probably anti-social, but even of that I am not sure. It's certainly unwise and can lead to endless, incalculable trouble, but dishonest . . . no, I won't wear that. Anyway, what led you to this startling conclusion?'

'Well, you must admit that the basis of gambling, its lure if you like, is something for nothing. Money should be earned.'

'Except for a brief period when you worked at that Oxford Street store, you've never earned a shilling in your life. So, if something for nothing is dishonest, you must be as crooked as a dog's hind leg. Another thing . . . you haven't called me a bastard, a bloody fool or a silly bugger all the evening. Don't tell me you're crusading against bad language, too.'

'Bugger you, you sarcastic bastard!'

This was better, now we were on familiar ground.

Then she ruined it all by apologizing.

'The voice is the voice of Esmé,' I said, 'but I'll be damned if the words are hers.'

I was just bracing myself for a good old-fashioned brawl when she covered her face with her hands and began to bawl like an infant.

Now my experience of women who end discussions by taking refuge in tears is that they are inviting one to ask why. Well, I'd see her in hell before I asked. 'Take your time, have a good cry,' I said as I left, 'you'll feel better in the morning.'

When I returned from taking the dogs for a walk, she

159

had gone to bed. Alphonsine's only observation was: 'Pauvre mademoiselle!'

There was another brief encounter in the morning. 'Did anyone phone me last evening?' she asked.

'I don't know.'

'What do you mean . . . you don't know?'

'Exactly what I say.'

'But unless you were out all night, you must know whether the phone rang, or not.'

'That isn't what you asked me,' I told her. 'I rather think the phone did ring, but as I never answer it after 10 p.m., I have no idea who was on the other end of the line.'

'You mean,' she said aghast, 'that you let a phone ring when all you had to do was stretch out a hand to lift the receiver?'

'I mean,' I said coldly, 'that it's my phone and I do what the hell I like with it, or nothing at all, and while we are about it, life would be a lot easier for both of us if you made an effort to be polite, because if you don't. . . .'

'And if I don't?' she snarled.

As it was obvious what I was going to say, I left it unsaid.

'Well, anything more?' she said belligerently.

'Yes,' I said very quietly for emphasis, 'don't take that tone with me again. I won't take it. Give someone else the benefit of your foul temper. If you're in trouble, I'll try to help. If it's morning sickness, it's outside my field. If you're constipated, there's a bottle in my bathroom marked "Faith". Help yourself.'

'Why faith?'

'Because it's supposed to move mountains.'

'You bastard!'

After that we were friends again. Nevertheless, something was troubling her, something she was too embarrassed to talk about. As the French put it, she had *honte*, which lies between shame and shyness. When a man goes out of character, look for the woman. Esmé had gone so badly out of character that, somewhere in the background of her life, I was sure a man was lurking, a man with enough influence over her to put into her mouth words of a kind that would never have come to her spontaneously. Unless she had been faintly ashamed of him, she would have spoken openly about him. Esmé had few inhibitions to hamper her.

In most matters I believe I am better than averagely observant, but my blind spot, or one of them, is clothes. Unless clothes, male or female, are dirty, torn or completely outrageous, I seldom notice them. Within limits, I suppose, I don't regard them as important. Clothes are, when one reflects upon the matter, a kind of protective colouring. To be well dressed, therefore, a man should be inconspicuous, but I am not at all sure that this applies to women, although logically it should apply to both.

Let that be as it may, for I don't want to dogmatize about it, I became aware over a considerable period of time that Esmé looked different, from which point I applied myself to ascertaining in what way. The penny dropped finally when I remembered that until recently she had always worn bright colours and, incidentally, looked well in them. Now, suddenly, she was becoming almost drab in appearance, favouring beige, grey, and other subdued shades.

Everything about her, I now realized, was toned down to some new standard. Except in moments of great stress her lurid language had lost all its vigour. Although the word as applied to Esmé sounds quite absurd, there was about her an air of resignation and placidity more appropriate to a convent.

'Why are you staring at me?' she asked one day.

'I'm trying to work out why you have started to dress as though you were applying for the job of nursery governess in the household of a Presbyterian divine. What has happened to the vivid shades, reds and blues you used to wear . . . and wear so well?'

The answer to this was a shrug.

'That blouse you're wearing doesn't look like you at all,' I went on.

'In what way?'

161

'For one thing,' I told her, 'it doesn't reveal so much breast meat. . . .'

'What a disgusting expression!'

'I've heard you use many far worse,' I told her.

Seeing that I was wasting my time, I asked her whether she would be in for dinner that evening. 'Yes, if you promise not to cross-question me.'

She brought a poor appetite to a good dinner. As I remember it, we began with a dish of *rougets* . . . the baby red mullet about the size of large sardines . . . *meunière*, really swimming in butter. She picked at them, which annoyed me. This was followed by beef olives, a dish in which Alphonsine excels. We were given eight rolls of thinly cut buttock steak, as it is called in England. Esmé ate one. I seldom eat sweets, but in deference to Esmé we had a *soufflé* flavoured with kirsch. She condescended to eat a little of it.

Since it was implicit in her presence that I could not question her at all, since I did not know which were the forbidden areas, there wasn't much conversation.

'I had a long talk with Father Delorme today,' she announced out of the blue. 'I find myself wondering whether he is as wise as you seem to think he is.'

'I regard him as a truly wise old man, even if loaded with prejudice and not always well informed. . . .'

'How can he be wise and not well informed?'

'Easily,' I replied. 'His knowledge of nuclear physics is nil and he is wise enough to know it, so he does not display his ignorance by talking nonsense on the subject. I imagine that it was not about nuclear physics that you consulted him. . . .'

'No, you stupid bugger,' she retorted, with a flash of her old courtesy, 'it was not. It was about my private—repeat private—life.'

'And was he able to help you?'

'No,' she snapped. 'If I do what he tells me to, I shall ruin this life entirely, whereas if I don't I shall ruin the next. What would you do?'

162

'Toss a coin, of course. It might, just might, fall on its edge and stay there.'

'I'm desperately unhappy, Steve, but you seem to think there is something funny about it.'

'The basis of all humour is supposed to be somebody else's misfortunes,' I reminded her. 'Try laughing at yourself. Laughter is a wonderful solvent, and no matter what your particular troubles are, you can be sure that ten million other women have been through them ... and survived.'

She was not very far from tears, so I broke it up.

It was that same evening, as I remember it, that a friend phoned me and happened to mention that János and a new partner had enjoyed a phenomenal run of luck the previous day. This was my first intimation that János had found someone to replace Esmé. I passed on the news to Esmé at cocktail time. She did not seem best pleased. 'Do you know who she is?' she asked me. I told her I knew nothing more than the bare fact.

The next thing I knew was seeing Esmé's car disappearing down the road in a cloud of dust. Assuming, and rightly, that she would not be back in time for dinner, I asked someone else to join me. It was, incidentally, a good dinner. Although quite beside the point, it is worthy of mention. There are not so many good meals in life that one can afford to slight them. Ordinarily speaking, I find a guinea fowl just about the least interesting creature that sprouts feathers, but Alphonsine has a way with them. Instead of being dry, tough and tasteless, they emerge from her kitchen juicy, tender and full of flavour. It was almost Esmé's favourite dish and had been ordered at her special request.

I turned in just before ten o'clock. At 10.20 the phone rang. At 11.45 a car arrived in the drive. I assumed it was Esmé, and as I was only reading I got up specially to tell her about the excellence of the guinea fowl she had missed. When I opened the door it was to find János standing there. 'I suppose you know what happened this evening,' he said breathlessly.

163

I shook my head.

'My partner and I were in the middle of the best winning streak we have ever known,' he began, 'when Esmé arrived on the scene like a madwoman. My partner's face had three deep vertical scratches before he had time to realize what was happening. At the top of her voice she called us "Tricky, double-crossing Hungarian bastards." Can you imagine that?'

'Yes, easily.'

'Then she slapped the face of one of the staff who was trying to keep her quiet. She doesn't shush to order. After a bit of a struggle, all three of us were put out and told never to come back. Once outside, Peter made a run for his car, jumped into it and drove west at a terrific speed with Esmé just behind him. I thought perhaps they might be here. . . .'

'Why would your partner come here?' I asked irritably. 'I don't even know the bloody man.'

'Of course you know him. You and I and Peter Kun dined together . . . surely you remember?'

'Yes, of course I remember, but how was I to know that his name was Peter or that he was your partner? More than that, why should Esmé try to scratch his eyes out. I didn't know they knew each other. The time Kun dined with us Esmé went home with the sulks.'

'Well,' said János uncomfortably, 'I happen to know that they have been seeing quite a lot of each other, and I gather from Peter that until this evening she believed he was in Paris on business.'

The plot thickened.

'I just hope they haven't got killed on the Autoroute,' said János. 'Esmé is a terrible driver at any time and Peter isn't much better.'

As there seemed nothing to do, I went to bed, offering János the spare room if he wanted it. As he wanted to continue the search for the other two, he drove off.

Either I guessed then, or was told later, or a mixture of the two, that Kun was the root cause of Esmé's tears. But

164

it soon became apparent that such was the case. Esmé had succumbed to the Kun charm. That was as understandable as it was obvious. But what was less easy to understand was why she had abandoned her extremely profitable gambling partnership with János. Still less why she had evidently made a great effort to clean up her vocabulary and dress dowdily in harmony with her new mealy-mouthed mode of expression. No theory I could formulate would fit the facts as I knew them. The truth, as it usually does, emerged in due time and was as improbable as the protagonists themselves.

Here, as nearly as I have been able to sort them out, are the facts. Esmé met Kun either just before or just after I did. The attraction was mutual, but I think she fell for him harder than he did for her. He was so accustomed to women making asses of themselves over him that he had come to take it for granted. In Esmé, it seems safe to say, he saw not only a most attractive girl-friend but, more important, a way out of most, if not all, his difficulties.

The first and most necessary step was to persuade Esmé that she was too fine and pure to risk contamination in the loose atmosphere of a gambling hell. However profitable it might be, it was an unworthy way of earning a living. Where else but in such a place could she have learned to use such horrifying language? Soon, all too soon, unless she mended her ways, she would become like the greedy old crones who hovered on the fringe of gambling. He must have piled it on and on and on, for she swallowed it whole and our Esmé, let me add, was far from being the vain, empty-headed, gullible girl who might have been expected to swallow such hokum.

The reason behind all this elaborate flimflam was as dark and devious as a Hungarian coalmine, if they have coalmines in Hungary. It was, simply, that if Esmé could be persuaded to abandon her partnership with János, his old friend János would welcome him with open arms as a substitute. Money would come rolling in and most of the pressing problems would vanish. What had to be avoided at all costs was a confrontation with Esmé in the casino, for having expressed himself so strongly on the subject, his own presence there would be hard to explain. So, to reduce the chances of this happening, he extracted from Esmé a solemn promise never to set foot in a casino again.

Like the best of schemes, it had its little weaknesses, but all in all it was an expert job which gave him several undisturbed weeks as János's partner, enabling him to pay his hotel bill, buy an expensive car and, generally speaking, live the life of Reilly. At first it was necessary to see Esmé daily in order to make sure that she was still securely under his influence, but when this became somewhat tedious, he invented important business in Paris to account for his defection.

That, as nearly as I can piece it all together, is the story up to Esmé's discovery of Kun's perfidy and the brawl in the casino, followed by Kun's flight in his own car and her hot pursuit.

Now Esmé, as has been made apparent already, was a somewhat hot-tempered young woman. Chartrain, who witnessed the casino brawl was charitable enough when talking about it afterwards to call it 'high-spirited'. As there were no witnesses of the scene when she caught up with Kun near Brignolles, the details must be left to our imaginations, although it is safe to say that it must have been a brisk encounter. Then they disappeared for several days and when, finally, they came up for air, they arrived in Ste Monique hand in hand looking extremely pleased with life and with each other.

Among the letters which had arrived for Esmé was one announcing that her divorce had gone through. If I had known its contents I would have dropped it in the incinerator, for it could not have arrived at a less opportune moment.

János, who arrived on the scene after a phone call to say that the wanderers had returned, seemed to accept the situation philosphically, so philosophically indeed that Esmé regarded herself as having been insulted and, furthermore, told him so. 'You bloody Hungarians!' was her comparatively mild observation.

'Don't forget that Peter is a Hungarian too,' János warned her.

That gave her food for thought.

Esmé had the gall to ask me whether it would be all right if Peter Kun moved into the guest cottage and was miffed when I refused to entertain the idea. Truth to tell, I heaved a sigh of relief when I was once more left to myself. The three of them were too much for me.

*　　*　　*　　*

At Nice airport, where I had been waiting two hours for the plane to Geneva, my attention was attracted to a gigantic, splendidly handsome negro clad in an ankle-length gown of many colours. He was, if ever I saw one, a genial rascal who had managed to salvage a great natural dignity from life. Here, it was plain to see, was a man with access to scads of money. Being lost in speculation about the man, it was some while before I realized that the little man trotting along beside him was none other than Peter Kun. I don't think he recognized me, but if he did he probably had his good reasons for not appearing to do so. They were such an incongruous pair that my curiosity was aroused. It was soon satisfied.

The African and Kun travelled on the same plane as I was on . . . first class, of course. From the way they were treated on arrival at Geneva, the African had to be someone of importance. The following morning's newspaper enlightened me. A photograph of them was captioned: 'His Excellency President Karimba of M'Bongoland and Monsieur Kun, his newly appointed Hungarian financial adviser.'

Both the name of the President and his country are here fictitious. What I have called M'Bongoland is one of the new African republics which have appeared since colonialism was swept away.

The episode gave me much food for thought. I do not know M'Bongoland and, please God, never will, but my heartfelt sympathy went out to its unhappy people. My own country, despite its strongly entrenched financial institutions and high reputation for stability, suffered enough from Hungarian financial genius. What, I asked myself, would be the impact of Peter Kun on this unfortunate republic's already tottering economy? The answer was too fraught with weird possibilities to contemplate.

17

When I reached home after the brief visit to Geneva, I was greeted by Alphonsine with the news that mademoiselle was installed in the guest cottage. She hoped it was all right. I hoped so, too, but doubted it.

At dinner that evening it transpired that Esmé also had been at the airport when Peter Kun had flown out. She confirmed the newspaper story I had read in Geneva. 'It is a wonderful opportunity for Peter,' she told me, 'and I think he was so wise to jump at it. He had another offer at the same time from a firm called Interpol, but he preferred to go to Africa.'

'How did he happen to meet the President of M'Bongoland?' I asked.

'János introduced him. Karimba has only been President for a short time and János knew him when he was military attaché somewhere. It may not turn out well, of course, but if it doesn't, Peter can always fall back on the Interpol offer.'

'Yes, I was forgetting that. Good old Interpol!'

'You sound as though you don't believe me,' said Esmé, 'but it's quite true. Peter is a very talented man.'

'But I do believe you,' I assured her, 'especially the bit about Interpol.'

'Do you know them then?' she asked eagerly.

'Not personally, only by repute.'

Sooner or later the scales of disillusionment were going to fall from those lovely eyes. Who was I to say whether it should be sooner rather than later?

'How do things stand between you and Peter?' I asked.

'We were going to get married at the end of the month, only Peter had to leave in such a hurry.'

'It's a pity he couldn't have waited long enough to let those scratches heal. Your fingernails must have been dipped in something particularly nasty. I caught a glimpse of his face at Nice airport. It was still a nasty mess.'

'He's got something to remember me by,' said Esmé, with a glint in her eyes. 'Now he knows what to expect if he plays monkey tricks with me. Meanwhile, the plan is for me to join him when he has had time to settle down. We shall be married out there. I suppose it's no use asking you to come, is it? It would be wonderful if you'd take Father's place and give me away.'

'No, thank you,' I said, 'but you can always count on me not to give you away.'

To be happy, even if only for a very brief spell, is something which some people seem never to achieve. Esmé was happy and I could not bring myself to be a prophet of gloom. All it would achieve for me would be to cost me a friend, and I have not so many that I can afford to be reckless with them. Besides, there was always the possibility, remote as it might be, that it would all turn out better than I feared it would. Lots of funny things could happen in a place like M'Bongoland, especially to a reckless fellow like Peter. While there were still lions, snakes and crocodiles, anything could happen. It was no use being too pessimistic. There was also the further thought that with Peter eliminated from the running, whether by wild beasts, beri-beri, bilharzia or Interpol, her genius for doing the wrong thing would inevitably make her choice fall on some equally unsuitable mate. After all, Peter was polite, amusing and, within a narrow field, talented, and by way of bonus possessing the Hungarian genius for survival. No, all was not lost.

'You haven't a very good opinion of Peter, have you?' she ventured.

'I have only met him once and that briefly,' I replied.

'You're hedging because you don't want to commit yourself. I know you, Steve.'

'My dear Esmé, I am sitting astride the fence so firmly

that I shall be scarred for life. Don't waste time trying to make me lose my balance.'

For the next couple of weeks Esmé was able to extract some meagre satisfaction from the thought that in far-off M'Bongoland Peter, busy as a bird-dog, was making a home for them. By the third week this, as a source of comfort, began to wear thin. Her theme song then was: 'Why doesn't the bugger write?' As the third week melted into the fourth, she spent the hour after the postman's arrival tapping a dainty foot on the tiled floors. If 'baleful' means what I think it does, there was a baleful look in her eyes. Then, on the distinct understanding that she would pay for the calls, she initiated a telephone siege of the Presidential Palace in M'Bara, the capital. Here, from a sleepy telephone operator, she was given a number where Peter could be reached. After several attempts a dulcet voice, also somewhat sleepy, answered the phone.

Esmé, sitting quietly on the telephone stool, suddenly reacted like a spring-operated jack-in-the-box. It was, of course, an illusion, but she appeared to hit the ceiling in her mad gyrations. 'The black-hearted Hungarian bastard!' she screamed. 'I'll cut his bloody throat, so help me. What do you think that bitch said to me? *"Pierre, chéri, c'est toi?"* '

'What else?'

'Wasn't that enough?'

'But you shouldn't be surprised at her talking French,' I told her, 'because M'Bongoland, before it changed its name and became an independent republic, was a French colony. French is still probably the official language. . . .'

'Bloody funny, bloody funny!'

'What next?' I asked.

'What next?' she echoed shrilly. 'I'll tell you what next. I'm taking the first plane to whatsitsname and God help him and that'—she stopped abruptly as a new thought struck her —'What colour do you suppose she is?'

'Now, now!' I chided her gently. 'If M'Bongoland is to be your future home, you must make up your mind to leave all your racial prejudices behind you. What does it matter

171

what colour she is, so long as she was brought up to observe good Christian principles?'

'I'll give her good Christian principles,' she said darkly, 'and if she isn't black and blue now, she will be by the time I've finished with her. I should have known better than to let that tricky bastard out of my sight.'

It was more than a week before Esmé was able to secure an air passage to join Peter and even then it was a circuitous route. It was—I speak for myself—a disturbed and disturbing week, for Esmé's rage had a threatening presence of its own. It was like living with a steam boiler hissing at the seams, waiting for it to burst and destroy everything within range. When she approached them, the dogs cowered, the cat spat and even Alphonsine, Esmé's ardent admirer, admitted to me with masterly under-statement that *'mademoiselle est un peu difficile.'*

The regrets I expressed at her departure didn't sound very convincing, even to me. I felt conscious that the sands of obligation to an old friend were running out. When the plane taking her to Africa was airborne, I turned away and, thankfully, let her drop from mind.

But not for long.

There was something sinister in the way Alphonsine greeted me on my return home. She adopts an unpleasing crab crawl when she is the bearer of bad news. 'Evidently, mademoiselle does not intend to stay long in Africa,' she announced.

'What makes you say that?' I asked, with a sinking feeling.

'She has left almost all her clothes and other belongings in the cottage. Also a list of the things she wants pressed.'

'Pack everything and do not trouble about the pressing,' I told her. 'Things will change here,' I added darkly.

Then there arose the question of what to do with Esmé's expensive new car which had been serviced and was delivered by the garage that afternoon. I have garage space for two cars, one a battered old station wagon and the other a fairly new car. Having gone to the expense of having a double garage, I was damned if I would let one of my cars stand out in all weathers.

I told the garage to take back Esmé's car and not to put the storage charges, or any other charges, on to my bill. The time had come to assert myself.

At breakfast one morning I found myself wondering what had happened to János now that every casino on the coast was closed to him. I had not long to wonder. He phoned during the morning, more or less inviting himself to lunch.

'And how is the famous Hungarian astrologer?' I asked when greetings were over.

'If I had not been invited by Peter to join him,' János replied, 'I was seriously considering setting up as an astrologer. In fact, I may do so anyway. It has great possibilities.'

'What in hell do you know about astrology?' I asked.

'Nothing . . . nothing at all, but I still have my nose.'

'Don't tell me now that you can stick your nose out into space and smell the stars, for while I will admit that you Hungarians are a remarkable people. . . .'

'Will you not understand that even if I told people the truth, that I obtain my results through my nose, they would not believe me. But if I tell them the lie that I read their fortunes by the stars, they will believe me, and even if I do not know one end of a horoscope from another, there is nothing to stop me from calling myself an astrologer.

'You see, although Chartrain won't ever let me play in the casino again, we are still good friends and he, you may believe me, has given me a tremendous reputation as an astrologer.'

I just grunted. János has a way of making the most improbable things sound reasonable and credible.

'What's all this about going to join Peter Kun?' I asked. 'Are they short of astrologers and witch doctors in M'Bongoland?'

'I have nothing definite in mind,' János replied airily, 'but Peter writes to say there are great possibilities and, after all, being financial adviser to the President, he should know.'

173

'I suppose he learned high finance at the same school where you learned astrology, is that it?'

'Something like that,' he replied, with an evil grin.

I wondered when he would come to the point of his visit, but I need not have done. It was just a friendly call and János whatever else he may be—and he is many things —is a friendly fellow.

Then we discussed Esmé and Peter Kun. 'Just exactly what is meant by financial adviser to the President?' I asked.

'Well, you know Peter. . . .'

'But I don't,' I reminded him. 'I met him once.'

'Peter's job, as I understand it, is to raise more revenue. Like all these ex-colonies,' János went on, 'M'Bongoland is learning that freedom includes the freedom to go broke. The country is full of unfinished roads, half-built hospitals and schools, broken down railways and that sort of thing. The only new building completed since independence is the President's palace, which cost a little more than the $20,000,000 lent by the Americans for flood control. Peter says it is first class. He has a ten-room apartment there. . . .'

I listened, fascinated, as snippets of information emerged about the new life Peter Kun was carving for himself in the wilds of Africa. I marvelled too, at the amazing adaptability and versatility of these Hungarians who, their own country in ruins under the heel of a conqueror, were able to find their niches wherever they went. I knew one Hungarian who, while he was in process of learning the English language, wrote a novel in English which, when his knowledge of the language had improved, he polished up and sold to a publisher.

Two days later, Africa had swallowed János Tisza, too. Soon, I felt, that vast Continent would begin to vibrate.

*   *   *   *

As they always do when I see Esmé's handwriting on an envelope, my hands began to tremble. I let the letter lie on my desk unopened until the evening of the next day. I opened it with my second brandy-and-soda :

174

M'Bara, Wednesday.

No date, of course.

Dear Steve: Well, here I am and none too soon. Now the dust has begun to settle I can find time to write. I found on arrival that my worst fears were realized, but I soon settled *her* hash and kicked her cute little arse down two flights of the Palace stairs.

The tall man—for the future let us call him Mr Smith, it's safer—is rather a pet. He has taken a great shine to Peter. That's fine, but what *is* just a wee bit worrying is that he appears to have taken a shine to *me*. Fortunately, I get on like a house on fire with Mrs Smith. She would stand 6 ft 7 in. in her socks if she ever wore them. Hitherto, she has worn nothing but Paris models in which she looks like hell. I have persuaded her to go back to native costume in which she looks simply smashing. Mr Smith approves.

I don't understand finance, but Peter seems to. He says the country is in a bad way, but that things are bound to improve when a new consignment of banknotes arrives from the printer next week.

János is here. He told me he saw you before he left. He is already up to the neck in work. He has persuaded Mr Smith to let him organize a *Loterie Nationale* on the lines of the French one. It will raise a lot of revenue. Peter is working out the details for having income-tax for the first time. It won't make him very popular.

Monday.

I've been doing some thinking. What's the use of having income-tax when, so far as I can learn, nobody has any income except Mr Smith and a few of his pals. Peter says it's for foreigners who are skimming the wealth of the country. What wealth? I've not seen any ... outside the Palace, of course.

The two big snags here are the climate, which is bloody, and the cooking which is worse. The cook, who read in a book that Hungarians eat goulash, served goulash for dinner last night. Mr Smith loved it, but when he told us it was monkey goulash, I threw up.

When I think of Alphonsine I drool. I suppose you wouldn't

let her come out here? She'd be paid any wage she asked. Peter would only have to order some more money to be printed.

Letters from Esmé came in a steady stream, suggesting to me that she was lonely and in need of a confidant. My imagination being too vivid for comfort, I tried not to dwell on the incalculable possibilities now that the financial affairs of M'Bongoland had passed into Hungarian hands. I won't quote the letters *in extenso* because they were wearisome and tended to be repetitive. Instead, I will confine myself to quoting odd paragraphs which tend to shed light on the progress of events. Here is a sample which suggests that the 6 ft. 7 in. Mrs Smith had limitations as a companion:

Mrs S. is becoming a bloody bore. All she can talk about is the love potions she gets from an old crone in the country. It seems that Mr S. is not being as attentive as he should. I am caught in a vicious circle. The best way of keeping him at bay is to spend as much time as possible with her when Peter isn't around.

Then there was another complication:

Although Mr S. is as promiscuous as a tomcat, the missionaries caught him young and he is a devout R.C. When Peter and I get married P. wants it to be a Cathedral wedding. Mr S. would put the seal of acceptance on us by being present in person. What P. forgets is that I am a divorced woman. If they knew that, the bishop wouldn't perform the ceremony and Mr S. wouldn't attend. I am not prepared to lie to the bishop about it. Now what?

The next letter contained an item of news which, I regret to say, did not take me by surprise:

János came round last evening for a drink. After sniffing me very carefully—a bit too carefully for Peter's liking—he pronounced that I was in a vein of extremely good luck. I said it was a pity there wasn't a casino in M'Bara. János retorted, rather darkly I thought, that casinos weren't the only places where luck was valuable. How right he was! Today was the first drawing of the *Loterie Nationale* and,

176

would you believe it, little Esmé won the first prize of three million bongos. What makes it a bit hard to understand is that I didn't buy a ticket. I found the winning ticket on my breakfast tray. These bloody Hungarians! Mr S. would have won the first draw only he thought it wouldn't look too well. But what bothers me is that he isn't going to let me forget that but for him I wouldn't have won. Now I shall have to live with Mrs S. in my hair.

Then, typical of Esmé, came the announcement that she had bought herself a $4\frac{1}{2}$–litre Semproni convertible which, it seemed, turned out a trifle disappointing:

There's nothing wrong with the car, which is a peach. The trouble is that there are so few roads, and those there are are choked with slow-moving traffic, masses of people walking in the middle, to say nothing of stray animals and sleeping dogs. Despite all the disadvantages of having Mr S. for a friend, and these I must leave to your imagination, I must say he turned up trumps in this case. I now have a gadget on the car, which instead of hooting gives off a rattle like a machine-gun and can be heard a mile ahead. The man has his humane side, for he asked me to try hard not to kill anyone. He explained that when too many people get killed on the roads it starts an epidemic of rock-throwing which is very unpopular with other motorists.

There is a sixty-mile stretch of fine tarmac road from the capital down to the coast. I took Mrs S. on the first run. She was thrilled. At ninety that car is just idling. I don't dare to put my foot down. When we got near the first village, I switched on the machine-gun gadget and by the time we reached it the entire damned population was up in the trees. It was like driving through an abandoned country. There was a sort of country club with a swimming pool at the beach, but Mrs S. was in a hurry to get back to the Palace so we didn't swim. It seems she gave Mr S. a double dose of the love potion and she didn't want to miss anything.

Later.

Peter and János are off on some monkey business they won't tell me about so, as you can imagine, it must be pretty off-colour. I've had an evening alone and, truth to tell, I've rather enjoyed it. I shall have to stop now because someone with heavy boots is trying to kick down the door. My God! If it's Mr Smith I shall have to phone *her* to come and rescue me. The door is beginning to splinter. . . .

The letter ended there like a serial melodrama. The strange thing is that it bore a Liverpool postmark. The next letter, dated two days later, bore a London postmark. Being short, I quote it all.

Dear Steve: I was seasick all the way from Port M'Bara to Liverpool, far too ill to write. You must have wondered what happened after my door had been kicked down. Well, thank God! it wasn't Mr You-know-who. It was the captain of the Palace Guard. I was safe with him because he's a roaring pansy. He came to say that there had been an attempted counter-revolution and that at His Excellency's orders I was to be taken immediately to the coast where a passage to England had been arranged for me. There was no time to pack anything other than necessities. As I was getting into the Landrover I heard Peter shouting. The driver wouldn't stop. Then I heard a shot and I feared the worst.

I am coming down straight away to Ste Monique to collect my car and other belongings, also to introduce someone to you. I met him aboard the ship. His name is ffoulkes and he has a slight stammer. He will have to change it, of course, but I haven't broken the news to him yet. It must have been the double-eff that caused the stammer in the first place.

I hope you'll be able to put me up for a day or so. T-t-tony can s-stay at a hotel. My God! I hope I don't catch it.

Love,

Esmé

When she heard the news, Alphonsine was delighted. I am glad someone was. But she was not best pleased when I told her not to unpack Esmé's valises. Well, approximately a week later, Esmé and T-t-tony ff-ffoulkes arrived in a minuscule car they had hired at Nice airport. He was a pleasant enough young man about whom the worst thing I can say is that he aroused in me neither admiration nor hostility. In fact, he aroused nothing.

I gathered in the first few minutes that he had been in Port M'Bara to visit an old friend and that he was an assistant master at a preparatory school owned by his father and which in the fullness of time he would, presumably, inherit.

While Esmé was off having a wash and brush up, he confided to me that he thought she was a j-j-jolly good sort. I knew what I thought, but had no wish to disillusion him. She'd been j-j-jolly brave about the whole thing.

On the way down to Port M'Bara the pansy Captain of the Palace Guard had told Esmé that Peter Kun had in fact been shot, but on the orders of the President, not by the counter-revolutionaries. 'Peter and János, poor darlings,' she explained, 'had advised the President to double the price of cigarettes sold by the Régie. But between them they worked a big fiddle, releasing fifty million cigarettes the day before the price rise and splitting the difference with the distributors, who would doubtless sell them at the new price. I forgot the exact details, but it was something like that. You know ... good, straight Hungarian business. Poor Peter! He was rather a darling, you know, despite everything.'

'Well, I'm sure he would be flattered to learn how quickly after hearing the fatal shot you managed to console yourself.' I couldn't resist the stab.

'You bastard!'

'Whwh-a-t was that?' said T-t-tony, unable to believe his ears.

I glanced at my watch. 'I hate to be the bearer of bad news,' I told her, 'but for your information Peter is giving a little dinner party at Roberto's in Cannes. It's a sort of celebration. He invited me, but I had a prior engagement. I believe it's quite a celebration.'

'Celebrating what?' asked Esmé in a quiet voice which positively quivered with rising indignation.

'It's to meet his fiancée. She's very rich, so he won't have to take that job with Interpol. If you hurry, you'll just have time to get there. I'm sure he and Tony would get along together splendidly.'

It really shook her to realize how badly she had under-estimated the Hungarian talent for survival.

Someone, I think it was Father Delorme, once called Esmé 'a somewhat impulsive young lady.' It was the *mot juste*. Between where she was sitting and the front door, she just had time to call Peter a deceitful Hungarian bastard while the wretched Tony, mouth dropped, gazed at her in astonishment as the small car tore up the gravel. 'Well, really!' was all he said.

He had had more shocks already than he could conveniently absorb, but he was due for one more and it seemed kinder not to keep him in suspense. 'W-where d-do you s-suppose sh-she went?' he asked after what seemed an interminable silence.

'To Cannes, I think.'

'Wh-when w-will sh-she be b-b-back?'

'I don't know. As you know, our Esmé is just a trifle unpredictable. But purely as an expression of opinion, I would judge never. On the other hand, of course, she might be back in a couple of hours. Why don't we get drunk while we're waiting?'

'That's a jolly good idea,' he said, so shocked that he forgot to stammer.

With the fifth or sixth brandy I think he believed me when I told him what a lucky escape he had had.

While Alphonsine was helping me to lay him out in the spare room she muttered—and for the last time in my hearing—'Pauvre mademoiselle!'

'Since you are dripping over with sympathy,' I suggested, 'spare some for this *pauvre monsieur*.'

When Esmé phoned me the next day our talk didn't go with a swing. 'Peter and I are getting married as soon as possible,' she announced.

I remained silent.

'Aren't you going to congratulate us?' she asked.

'No, Esmé, I am not. The fact is that I've used up

180

today's ration of congratulations on p-p-poor T-t-tony, who's had a very lucky escape.'

'May I speak to him, please?'

'No, I'm afraid you can't. He has just left.'

'Oh!'

'But I expect he's gone away feeling very grateful to you.'

'Whatever for?'

'The shock you g-gave him c-c-cured his st-stammer.'

There was a gentle click as the receiver the other end was replaced, followed by a silence which lasted many months.

POSTSCRIPT

'There is a postcard from mademoiselle,' said Alphonsine in a great state of excitement, handing me the mail. 'It is from Beirut. I wonder what she is doing there.'

I wondered that myself and went on wondering, because the postcard shed no light on the subject. There was not even an address. It read:

> Lovely climate. P. doing well. Why not come and visit us? V. welcome any time. Have you any news of darling János? Love, Esmé

I was glad to learn that Peter was doing well. Left to imagine what now engaged his talents and energies, I decided that he had opened a school of salesmanship for Levantine carpet vendors. Failing that, he would be in the magic carpet business. Why pay exorbitant air fares when our magic carpets take you anywhere?

Had I any news of darling János? she wanted to know.

Indeed I had. János chose a typically János way of letting me know that he had survived the revolutions, the financial blizzards and the President's disfavour in far-off M'Bongoland. A letter bearing the M'Bara postmark advised me from the headquarters of the *Loterie Nationale* that ticket No. 1873791 in my name had won a prize value 250,000 bongos. A few days later the ticket in question arrived in a plain envelope.

The bank, of whom I enquired the current value of the bongo, urged me not to get too excited about this windfall. It had been a longish time since they had had any bongo transactions. Events in the republic had not inspired much international confidence. Perhaps Hungarian financial advisers had had something to do with this regrettable state of affairs, I mused.

Anyway, it was an extremely nice gesture on the part of János and I appreciated it.

A further communication from the M'Bongoland Exchange Control advised me that, being a resident abroad, the lottery prize could not be remitted to me and could only be paid to me in person on presentation of the ticket.

Nothing I had heard about M'Bongoland, least of all the murky mysteries of monkey goulash, inspired me with a desire to go there.

Then another communication from Esmé. A letter this time:

Dear Steve: I've had no reply to my card, so I hope all is well with you. I shall be a grass widow for several months, P. likely to be absent on important business. . . .

It may have been uncharitable, but I wondered if that important business were connected with Interpol in any way. Were events catching up with him? Anyway, how could I have replied to the card when there was no address?

. . . so until he returns, I shall be rather lonely. Would I be imposing on your good nature if. . . ?.'

What good nature did she have in mind? How could she impose on it?

The letter merited a reply. I told her how pleased I was that all was well and that my own plans involved foreign travel for an indefinite period. I permitted myself to read her a little homily about the unwisdom of long separations between young married couples. Unsatisfactory as it must have been to the recipient, it was better than the truth which was, simply, that I did not feel strong enough for another prolonged visit.

She is a dear girl and I am devoted to her, but she is not a restful guest. Drama seems to follow her like her shadow.

From Esmé my thoughts turned to other guests who have stayed with me, guests who had caused no trouble, had never been in the least inconsiderate or unreasonable, who had been in short so damned dull that their comings and goings had passed almost without notice. Wherever she was Esmé managed to raise hell, but she was alive and a part of life. . . .

Hastily thrusting these weak thoughts from me, I put my letter aside to be posted later.

Then there was János. I would feel happier about János when I learned that he had left M'Bongoland with a whole skin. I would feel happier about M'Bongoland, too. These small African states had enough troubles of their own without Hungarian financial advice, and while I won't go so far as to say that János was dishonest, there seemed to be a strong smell of fish about the *Loterie Nationale,* and if my not particularly acute olfactory sense could detect it, so presumably could those nearer to its source. Karimba alive, doubtless, was a valuable friend, but Karimba in exile with the hatchetmen hot on his trail, less so. My brief sight of him at the airport suggested that if the republic still had any portable wealth, it would soon follow the rest into a Swiss numbered account. Then how grateful would he be to his Hungarian adviser?

*   *   *   *

At a dinner party in Cannes I found myself next to an Englishwoman whose Christian name was Rosemary. We had known each other casually for many years since she spent a post-war summer in Ste Monique. Since then most of our encounters had been at the casino, where she seemed a consistent loser. She was charming but not over-burdened with brains.

'How is the roulette wheel treating you?' I asked in order to make conversation.

'Very much better, thank you,' said Rosemary. 'I won a little more than twenty thousand francs last night. You know,' she went on, being one of those who use 'you knows' instead of commas, 'it all dates from meeting a most wonderful man, an astrologer, who tells me when to play and when not to. When he tells me to play, I win. When he tells me not to play, I lose. It's as simple as that. . . .'

'But if he's so good, why play when he tells you not to?' I asked.

'You know the answer to that as well as I do,' she replied sadly. 'I can't help it. If I don't play, I sit miserably at home twisting handkerchiefs into shreds, imagining the coups I am missing. If only I could obey him, all my worries would be over. But it isn't his fault. He really is a wonderful man and shockingly expensive . . . a hundred francs a consultation. About the same as Harley Street, you know. He must be simply coining money, you know. He turns away clients in droves. That shows you how independent he is. Do you know that new apartment block on the lower slopes of Californie . . . the Palais Edouard VII? Well, you know, he has a huge penthouse apartment there. That tells its own story, you know, because even the titsy little apartments cost a fortune.'

'What is his name, this paragon?'

'He calls himself Professor Nemesis, but I don't expect that is his real name. He's quite young, not good looking, you know, but sort of ugly attractive. He doesn't really call himself an astrologer . . . astral science he calls it. There's something quite thrilling and sinister about him, you know. He gives me the creeps sometimes. He has a way of coming quite close to you as though he were about to kiss you. Then he appears to change his mind and sheers away. . . .'

'How very disappointing!' I said. 'Tell me, what nationality is he?'

'He's either a Czech or a Hungarian, I forget which. If he's a Czech, he hates Hungarians and vice versa. Does it matter?'

'To a Czech or a Hungarian, yes it does.'

There was little doubt in my mind that Professor Nemesis was a Hungarian, or that his given name was János. Just to resolve all doubt, I asked : 'Does he object to his clients wearing perfume?'

'Indeed, yes, and he won't allow smoking either. He says that tobacco smoke, perfumes and highly seasoned foods make it difficult for him because they cut the astral rays. Do you know what that means?'

'I know what it means, but I mustn't monopolize you by explaining. It would take a long time and I'm neglecting the plain woman on my left.'

I don't think I ever doubted that János, in the fullness of time, would land on his feet, but I wasn't prepared for the magnificently vulgar opulence of his penthouse apartment, or the luscious receptionist who dominated the foyer. To approach her one had to cross a really beautiful circular rug at least twenty feet in diameter, woven into which were the Signs of the Zodiac.

'The Professor asks me to apologize to you,' said the receptionist. 'Can I get you something to drink while you are waiting.'

'Mademoiselle,' I assured her, 'I do not mind how long I wait so long as I may sit here and look at you.'

She didn't look pleased or annoyed at this heavy-handed compliment. In fact, she didn't look anything. She was so used to compliments, I feel, that they just rolled off her.

Taking a seat close to the door of what seemed to be the *sanctum sanctorum,* I was privileged to eavesdrop on János and his client, whose voices were clearly audible—I believed purposely so and for my benefit—through a partly drawn curtain.

'I am not God, madame,' he was saying. 'If it is in your destiny to lose at the tables tonight, I cannot make you win. I cannot influence your play in the smallest degree. All I can do is to tell you whether, if you play, you will win or lose. So far I have not been wrong, have I? Have you lost faith in me? If so, you must on no account come here again. . . .'

'No, Professor, I have complete faith in you. It has never wavered.'

'Then, let me tell you again, if you play tonight you will lose. You have paid me a large fee to tell you the truth. There have been other nights when, despite the warning that you would lose, you have played and lost. Why come to me at all if you are going to disregard my advice?'

'*Professeur, c'est plus fort que moi!*' she said tearfully.

'Madame,' said János sternly, 'it gives me pain to have to speak to you so plainly, but you are not being fair to me. You are known as a client of mine. I forbid ... yes, I forbid you to lose money in public.'

The lady swept out.

Greetings over, János said: 'There, if you have never met one, is a specimen of the genus "compulsive gambler". They are strange, unhappy people. But who am I to complain? Because of them I live richly....'

'And have a sumptuously beautiful receptionist,' I added.

'... and many other blessings for which I am properly grateful. The case history of that poor woman is the case history of all my clients. When I tell them they will win, they win. When I tell them they will lose, they lose. All they need do is stay at home on those evenings, and if they did that, winning only when I tell them they will win, they would soon bankrupt the casinos. Why are they so foolish? I will tell you, my friend. Being compulsive gamblers, they gamble in order to lose. When they win money, they do not see the money in terms of what it will buy, a new suit, a new motor-car, a piece of jewellery. No, that would be waste. Money when he wins it is to the compulsive gambler merely a stepping stone to ten times more money. The advice I give them is honest advice. They pay me well, but ignore my advice. It is very sad,' he added, smiling his inscrutable smile.

As often before, I was tempted to write it all off as Hungarian flim-flam. But there was too much tangible evidence that out of the flimsy stuff of moonbeams he had created around him this ostentatious monument to human gullibility.

'I congratulate you, János,' I felt compelled to say. 'But what happens when this blows up?'

'As always, I shall follow my nose.'